P9-BIC-210

Also by Grace Paley

The Little Disturbances of Man

Enormous Changes at the Last Minute

Later the Same Day

GRACE PALEY

LATER THE
SAME DAY

Farrar Straus Giroux

NEW YORK

Copyright © 1985 by Grace Paley
All rights reserved
First printing, 1985
Printed in the United States of America
Published simultaneously in Canada by Collins Publishers, Toronto
Designed by Cynthia Krupat
Library of Congress Cataloging in Publication Data
Paley, Grace.
Later the same day.
I. Title.
PS3566.A46L3   1985   813'.54   84-26072

Some of the stories in this book appeared originally, in
slightly different form, in *The American Review, Fiction,
Harbinger, Heresies, Mother Jones, Ms., New England Review,
Poets and Writers, Three Penny Review,* and *Transatlantic Review.*
"Friends," "Love," and "Somewhere Else" first appeared in
The New Yorker.

*For my daughter and son, Nora and Danny,
without whom my life and literature
would be pretty slim*

and for Laura, our newest person

Love

First I wrote this poem:

Walking up the slate path of the college park
under the nearly full moon   the brown oak leaves
*   are red as maples*
and I have been looking at the young people
they speak and embrace one another
because of them I thought I would descend
into remembering love   so   I let myself down
*   hand over hand*
until my feet touched the earth of the gardens
of Vesey Street

I told my husband, I've just written a poem about
love.

What a good idea, he said.

Then he told me about Sally Johnson on Lake
Winnipesaukee, who was twelve and a half when he

was fourteen. Then he told me about Rosemarie Johanson on Lake Sunapee. Then he told me about Jane Marston in Concord High, and then he told me about Mary Smythe of Radcliffe when he was a poet at Harvard. Then he told me about two famous poets, one fair and one dark, both now dead, when he was a secret poet working at an acceptable trade in an office without windows. When at last he came to my time—that is, the past fifteen years or so—he told me about Dotty Wasserman.

Hold on, I said. What do you mean, Dotty Wasserman? She's a character in a book. She's not even a person.

O.K., he said. Then why Vesey Street? What's that?

Well, it's nothing special. I used to be in love with a guy who was a shrub buyer. Vesey Street was the downtown garden center of the city when the city still had wonderful centers of commerce. I used to walk the kids there when they were little carriage babies half asleep, maybe take the ferry to Hoboken. Years later I'd bike down there Sundays, ride round and round. I even saw him about three times.

No kidding, said my husband. How come I don't know the guy?

Ugh, the stupidity of the beloved. It's you, I said. Anyway, what's this baloney about you and Dotty Wasserman?

Nothing much. She was this crazy kid who hung around the bars. But she didn't drink. Really it was for the men, you know. Neither did I—drink too much, I mean. I was just hoping to get laid once in a while or maybe meet someone and fall madly in love.

He is that romantic. Sometimes I wonder if loving me in this homey life in middle age with two sets of bedroom slippers, one a skin of sandal for summer and the other pair lined with cozy sheepskin—it must be a disappointing experience for him.

He made a polite bridge over my conjectures. He said, She was also this funny mother in the park, years later, when we were all doing that municipal politics and I was married to Josephine. Dotty and I were both delegates to that famous Kansas City National Meeting of Town Meetings. N.M.T.M. Remember? Some woman.

No, I said, that's not true. She was made up, just plain invented in the late fifties.

Oh, he said, then it was after that. I must have met her afterward.

He is stubborn, so I dropped the subject and went to get the groceries. Our shrinking family requires more coffee, more eggs, more cheese, less butter, less meat, less orange juice, more grapefruit.

Walking along the street, encountering no neighbor, I hummed a little up-and-down tune and continued jostling time with the help of my nice reconnoitering brain. Here I was, experiencing the old earth of Vesey Street, breathing in and out with more attention to the process than is usual in the late morning—all because of love, probably. How interesting the way it glides to solid invented figures from true remembered wraiths. By God, I thought, the lover is real. The heart of the lover continues; it has been propagandized from birth.

I passed our local bookstore, which was doing well, with *The Joy of All Sex* underpinning its prosperity. The owner gave me, a dependable customer of poorly advertised books, an affectionate smile. He was a great success. (He didn't know that three years later his rent would be tripled, he would become a sad failure, and the landlord, feeling himself brilliant, an outwitting entrepreneur, a star in the microeconomic heavens, would be the famous success.)

From half a block away I could see the kale in the grocer's bin, crumbles of ice shining the dark leaves. In interior counterview I imagined my husband's north-country fields, the late-autumn frost in the curly green. I began to mumble a new poem:

In the grocer's bin, the green kale shines
in the north country it stands
*   sweet with frost*
dark and curly in a garden of tan hay
and light white snow . . .

Light white . . . I said that a couple of questioning times. Suddenly my outside eyes saw a fine-looking woman named Margaret, who hadn't spoken to me in two years. We'd had many years of political agreement before some matters relating to the Soviet Union separated us. In the angry months during which we were both right in many ways, she took away with her to her political position and daily friendship my own best friend, Louise—my lifelong park, P.T.A., and antiwar-movement sister, Louise.

In a hazy litter of love and leafy green vegetables I saw Margaret's good face, and before I remembered our serious difference, I smiled. At the same moment, she knew me and smiled. So foolish is the true lover when responded to that I took her hand as we passed, bent to it, pressed it to my cheek, and touched it with my lips.

I described all this to my husband at suppertime. Well of course, he said. Don't you know? The smile was for Margaret but really you do miss Louise a lot and the kiss was for Louise. We both said, Ah! Then we talked over the way the SALT treaty looked more like a floor than a ceiling, read a poem written by one of his daughters, looked at a TV show telling the destruction of the European textile industry, and then made love.

In the morning he said, You're some lover, you know. He said, You really are. You remind me a lot of Dotty Wasserman.

Dreamer in a
Dead Language

The old are modest, said Philip. They tend not to outlive one another.

That's witty, said Faith, but the more you think about it, the less it means.

Philip went to another table where he repeated it at once. Faith thought a certain amount of intransigence was nice in almost any lover. She said, Oh well, O.K. . . .

Now, why at that lively time of life, which is so full of standing up and lying down, *why* were they thinking and speaking sentences about the old.

Because Faith's father, one of the resident poets of the Children of Judea, Home for the Golden Ages, Coney Island Branch, had written still another song. This amazed nearly everyone in the Green Coq, that self-mocking tavern full of artists, entrepreneurs, and working women. In those years, much like these, amazing poems and grizzly tales were coming from the third grade, from the first grade in fact, where the children of many of the drinkers and talkers were learning creativity. But the old! This is very interesting, said some. This is too much, said others. The entrepreneurs said, Not at all—watch it —it's a trend.

Jack, Faith's oldest friend, never far but usually distant, said, I know what Philip means. He means the old are modest. They tend not to outlive each other by too much. Right, Phil?

Well, said Philip, you're right, but the mystery's gone.

In Faith's kitchen, later that night, Philip read the poem aloud. His voice had a timbre which reminded her of evening, maybe nighttime. She had often thought of the way wide air lives and moves in a man's chest. Then it's strummed into shape by the short-stringed voice box to become a wonderful secondary sexual characteristic.

Your voice reminds me of evening too, said Philip. This is the poem he read:

There is no rest for me since love departed
no sleep since I reached the bottom of the sea
and the end of this woman, my wife.
My lungs are full of water. I cannot breathe.
Still I long to go sailing in spring among realities.
There is a young girl who waits in a special time and
*   place*
to love me, to be my friend and lie beside me all
*   through the night.*

Dreamer in a Dead Language

Who's the girl? Philip asked.

Why, my mother of course.

You're sweet, Faith.

Of course it's my mother, Phil. My mother, young.

I think it's a different girl entirely.

No, said Faith. It has to be my mother.

But Faith, it doesn't matter who it is. What an old man writes poems about doesn't really matter.

Well, goodbye, said Faith. I've known you one day too long already.

O.K. Change of subject, smile, he said. I really am *crazy* about old people. Always have been. When Anita and I broke up, it was those great Sundays playing chess with her dad that I missed most. They don't talk to me, you know. People take everything personally. I don't, he said. Listen, I'd love to meet your daddy *and* your mom. Maybe I'll go with you tomorrow.

We don't say mom, we don't say daddy. We say mama and papa, when in a hurry we say pa and ma.

I do too, said Philip. I just forgot myself. How about I go with you tomorrow. Damn it, I don't sleep. I'll be up all night. I can't stop cooking. My head. It's like a percolator. Pop! pop! Maybe it's my age, prime of life, you know. Didn't I hear that the father of your children, if you don't mind my mentioning it, is doing a middleman dance around your papa?

How about a nice cup of Sleepytime tea?

Come on Faith, I asked you something.

[*13*

Yes.

Well, I could do better than he ever dreams of doing. I know—on good terms—more people. Who's that jerk know? Four old maids in advertising, three Seventh Avenue models, two fairies in TV, one literary dyke . . .

Philip . . .

I'm telling you something. My best friend is Ezra Kalmback. He made a fortune in the great American Craft and Hobby business—he can teach a four-year-old kid how to make an ancient Greek artifact. He's got a system and the equipment. That's how he supports his other side, the ethnic, you know. They publish these poor old dreamers in one dead language—or another. Hey! How's that! A title for your papa. "Dreamer in a Dead Language." Give me a pen. I got to write it down. O.K. Faith, I give you that title free of charge, even if you decide to leave me out.

Leave you out of what? she asked. Stop walking up and down. This room is too small. You'll wake the kids up. Phil, why does your voice get so squeaky when you talk business? It goes higher and higher. Right now you're above high C.

He had been thinking printing costs and percentage. He couldn't drop his answer more than half an octave. That's because I was once a pure-thinking English major—but alas, I was forced by bad management, the thoughtless begetting of children, and the vengeance of alimony into low practicality.

Faith bowed her head. She hated the idea of giving up the longed-for night in which sleep, sex, and affection would take their happy turns. What will I do, she thought. How can you talk like that to me Philip? Vengeance . . . you really stink Phil. Me. Anita's old friend. Are you dumb? She didn't want to hit him. Instead her eyes filled with tears.

What'd I do now? he asked. Oh, I know what I did. I know exactly.

What poet did you think was so great when you were pure?

Milton, he said. He was surprised. He hadn't known till asked that he was lonesome for all that Latin moralizing. You know, Faith, Milton was of the party of the devil, he said. I don't think I am. Maybe it's because I have to make a living.

I like two poems, said Faith, and except for my father's stuff, that's all I like. This was not necessarily true, but she was still thinking with her strict offended face. I like, *Hail to thee blithe spirit bird thou never wert*, and I like, *Oh what can ail thee knight at arms alone and palely loitering*. And that's all.

Now listen Philip, if you ever see my folks, if I ever bring you out there, don't mention Anita Franklin—my parents were crazy about her, they thought she'd be a Ph.D. medical doctor. Don't let on you were the guy who dumped her. In fact, she said sadly, don't even tell me about it again.

Faith's father had been waiting at the gate for about half an hour. He wasn't bored. He had been discussing the slogan "Black Is Beautiful" with Chuck Johnson, the gatekeeper. Who thought it up, Chuck?

I couldn't tell you, Mr. Darwin. It just settled on the street one day, there it was.

It's brilliant, said Mr. Darwin. If we could've thought that one up, it would've saved a lot of noses, believe me. You know what I'm talking about?

Then he smiled. Faithy! Richard! Anthony! You said you'd come and you came. Oh oh, I'm not sarcastic—it's only a fact. I'm happy. Chuck, you remember my youngest girl? Faithy, this is Chuck in charge of coming and going. Richard! Anthony! say hello to Chuck. Faithy, look at me, he said.

What a place! said Richard.

A castle! said Tonto.

You are nice to see your grandpa, said Chuck. I bet he been nice to you in his day.

Don't mention day. By me it's morning. Right Faith? I'm first starting out.

Starting out where? asked Faith. She was sorry so much would have to happen before the true and friendly visit.

To tell you the truth, I was talking to Ricardo the other day.

That's what I thought, what kind of junk did he fill you up with?

Faith, in the first place don't talk about their father in front of the boys. Do me the favor. It's a rotten game. Second, probably you and Ricardo got the wrong chemistry.

Chemistry? The famous scientist. Is that his idea? How's his chemistry with you? Huh?

Well, he talks.

Is Daddy here? asked Richard.

Who cares? said Tonto, looking at his mother's face. We don't care much, do we Faith?

No no, said Faith. Daddy isn't here. He just spoke to Grandpa, remember I told you about Grandpa writing that poetry. Well, Daddy likes it.

That's a little better, Mr. Darwin said.

I wish you luck Pa, but you ought to talk to a few other people. I could ask someone else—Ricardo is a smart operator, I know. What's he planning for you?

Well Faithy, two possibilities. The first a little volume, put out in beautiful vellum, maybe something like vellum, you know, *Poems from the Golden Age* . . . You like that?

Ugh! said Faith.

Is this a hospital? asked Richard.

The other thing is like this. Faithy, I got dozens of songs, you want to call them songs. You could call them songs or poems, whatever, I don't know. Well, he had a good idea, to put out a book also with some other people here—a series—if not a book. Keller for instance is no slouch when it comes to poetry, but he's more like an epic poet, you know . . . When Israel was a youth, then I loved . . . it's a first line, it goes on a hundred pages at least. Madame Nazdarova, our editor from *A Bessere Zeit*—did you meet her?—she listens like a disease. She's a natural editor. It goes in her ear one day. In a week you see it without complications, no mistakes, on paper.

You're some guy, Pa, said Faith. Worry and tenderness brought her brows together.

Don't wrinkle up so much, he said.

Oh shit! said Faith.

Is this a hospital? asked Richard.

They were walking toward a wall of wheelchairs that rested in the autumn sun. Off to the right under a great-leaf linden a gathering of furious arguers were leaning—every one of them—on aluminum walkers.

Like a design, said Mr. Darwin. A beautiful sight.

Well, *is* this a hospital? Richard asked.

It looks like a hospital, I bet, sonny. Is that it?

A little bit, Grandpa.

A lot, be honest. Honesty, my grandson, is *one* of the best policies.

Richard laughed. Only one, huh Grandpa.

See, Faithy, he gets the joke. Oh, you darling kid. What a sense of humor! Mr. Darwin whistled for the joy of a grandson with a sense of humor. Listen to him laugh, he said to a lady volunteer who had come to read very loud to the deaf.

I have a sense of humor too Grandpa, said Tonto.

Sure sonny, why not. Your mother was a constant entertainment to us. She could take jokes right out of the air for your grandma and me and your aunt and uncle. She had us in stitches, your mother.

She mostly laughs for company now, said Tonto, like if Philip comes.

Oh, he's so melodramatic, said Faith, pulling Tonto's ear. What a lie . . .

We got to fix that up, Anthony. Your mama's a beautiful girl. She should be happy. Let's think up a good joke to tell her. He thought for about twelve seconds. Well, O.K. I got it. Listen:

There's an old Jew. He's in Germany. It's maybe '39, '40. He comes around to the tourist office. He looks at the globe. They got a globe there. He says, Listen, I got to get out of here. Where you suggest, Herr Agent, I should go? The agency man also looks at the globe. The Jewish man says, Hey, how about here? He points to America. Oh, says the agency man, sorry, no, they got finished up with their quota. Ts, says the Jewish man, so how about here? He points to France. Last train left already for there, too bad, too bad. Nu, then to Russia? Sorry, absolutely nobody they let in there at the present time. A few more places . . . the answer is always, port is closed. They got already too many, we got no boats . . . So finally the poor Jew, he's thinking he can't go anywhere on the globe, also he also can't stay where he is, he says oi, he says ach! he pushes the globe away, disgusted. But he got hope. He says, So this one is used up, Herr Agent. Listen—you got another one?

Oh, said Faith, what a terrible thing. What's funny about that? I hate that joke.

I get it, I get it, said Richard. Another globe. There is no other globe. Only one globe, Mommy? He had no place to go. On account of that old

Hitler. Grandpa, tell it to me again. So I can tell my class.

I don't think it's so funny either, said Tonto.

Pa, is Hegel-Shtein with Mama? I don't know if I can take her today. She's too much.

Faith, who knows? You're not the only one. Who can stand her? One person, your mama, the saint, that's who. I'll tell you what—let the boys come with me. I'll give them a quick rundown on the place. You go upstairs. I'll show them wonderful sights.

Well, O.K. . . . will you go with Grandpa, boys?

Sure, said Tonto. Where'll you be?

With Grandma.

If I need to see you about anything, said Richard, could I?

Sure, sonny boys, said Mr. Darwin. Any time you need your mama say the word, one, two, three, you got her. O.K.? Faith, the elevator is over there by that entrance.

Christ, I know where the elevator is.

Once, not paying attention, rising in the gloom of her troubles, the elevator door had opened and she'd seen it—the sixth-floor ward.

Sure—the incurables, her father had said. Then to comfort her: Would you believe it, Faithy? Just like the world, the injustice. Even here, some of us start on the top. The rest of us got to work our way up.

Ha ha, said Faith.

It's only true, he said.

He explained that incurable did not mean near

death necessarily, it meant, in most cases, just too
far from living. There were, in fact, thirty-year-old
people in the ward, with healthy hearts and satisfactory lungs. But they lay flat or curved by pain, or
they were tied with shawls into wheelchairs. Here
and there an old or middle-aged parent came every
day to change the sheets or sing nursery rhymes to
her broken child.

The third floor, however, had some of the charac-
teristics of a hotel—that is, there were corridors,
rugs, and doors, and Faith's mother's door was, as
always, wide open. Near the window, using up light
and the curly shadow of hanging plants, Mrs. Hegel-
Shtein was wide awake, all smiles and speedy looks,
knitting needles and elbows jabbing the air. Faith
kissed her cheek for the awful sake of her mother's
kindness. Then she sat beside her mother to talk and
be friends.

Naturally, the very first thing her mother said
was: The boys? She looked as though she'd cry.

No no, Ma, I brought them, they're with Pa a
little.

I was afraid for a minute . . . This gives us a
chance . . . So, Faithy, tell me the truth. How is it?
A little better? The job helps?

The job . . . ugh. I'm buying a new typewriter,
Ma. I want to work at home. It's a big investment,
you know, like going into business.

Faith! Her mother turned to her. Why should you
go into business? You could be a social worker for
the city. You're very good-hearted, you always worried about the next fellow. You should be a teacher,

you could be off in the summer. You could get a counselor job, the children would go to camp.

Oh, Ma . . . oh, damn it! . . . said Faith. She looked at Mrs. Hegel-Shtein, who, for a solid minute, had not been listening because she was counting stitches.

What could I do, Faithy? You said eleven o'clock. Now it's one. Am I right?

I guess so, said Faith. There was no way to talk. She bent her head down to her mother's shoulder. She was much taller and it was hard to do. Though awkward, it was necessary. Her mother took her hand—pressed it to her cheek. Then she said, Ach! what I know about this hand . . . the way it used to eat applesauce, it didn't think a spoon was necessary. A very backward hand.

Oh boy, cute, said Mrs. Hegel-Shtein.

Mrs. Darwin turned the hand over, patted it, then dropped it. My goodness! Faithy. Faithy, how come you have a boil on the wrist. Don't you wash?

Ma, of course I wash. I don't know. Maybe it's from worry, anyway it's not a boil.

Please don't tell me worry. You went to college. Keep your hands clean. You took biology. I remember. So wash.

Ma. For godsakes. I know when to wash.

Mrs. Hegel-Shtein dropped her knitting. Mrs. Darwin, I don't like to interfere, only it so happens your little kiddie is right. Boils on the wrist is the least from worry. It's a scientific fact. Worries what start long ago don't come to a end. You didn't realize. Only go in and out, in and out the heart a couple hundred times something like gas. I can see you don't believe me. Stubborn Celia Darwin. Sickness comes from trouble. Cysts, I got all over inside me since the Depression. Where the doctor could put a hand, Cyst! he hollered. Gallbladder I have since Archie married a fool. Slow blood, I got that when Mr. Shtein died. Varicose veins, with *hemorrhoids* and a crooked neck, I got when Mr. Shtein got social security and retired. For him that time nervousness from the future come to an end. For me it first began. You know what is responsibility? To keep a sick old man alive. Everything like the last supper before they put the man in the electric chair. Turkey. Pot roast. Stuffed kishkas, kugels all kinds, soups without an end. Oi, Faithy, from this I got arthritis and rheumatism from top to bottom. Boils on the wrist is only the beginning.

What you mean is, Faith said, what you mean is —life has made you sick.

If that's what I mean, that's what I mean.

Now, said Mr. Darwin, who was on his way to the roof garden with the boys. He had passed the room, stopped to listen; he had a comment to make. He repeated: Now! then continued, That's what I got against modern times. It so happens you're in the swim, Mrs. H. Psychosomatic is everything nowadays. You don't have a cold that you say, I caught it on the job from Mr. Hirsh. No siree, you got your cold nowadays from your wife, whose health is perfect, she just doesn't think you're so handsome. It might turn out that to her you were always a mutt. Usually then you get hay fever for life. Every August is the anniversary of don't remind me.

All right, said Mrs. Darwin, the whole conversation is too much. My own health doesn't take every lopsided idea you got in your head, Sid. Meanwhile, wash up a little bit extra anyway, Faith, all right? A favor.

O.K. Ma, O.K., said Faith.

What about me? said Mr. Darwin, when will I talk to my girl? Faithy, come take a little walk.

I hardly sat down with Mama yet.

Go with him, her mother said. He can't sit. Mr. Pins and Needles. Tell her, Sid, she has to be more sensible. She's a mother. She doesn't have the choice.

Please don't tell me what to tell her, Celia. Faithy, come. Boys, stay here, talk to your grandma. Talk to her friend.

Why not, boys. Mrs. Hegel-Shtein smiled and invited them. Look it in the face: old age! Here it comes, ready or not. The boys looked, then moved close together, their elbows touching.

Faith tried to turn back to the children, but her father held her hand hard. Faithy, pay no attention. Let Mama take care. She'll make it a joke. She has presents for them. Come! We'll find a nice tree next to a bench. One thing this place got is trees and benches. Also, every bench is not just a bench—it's a dedicated bench. It has a name.

From the side garden door he showed her. That bench there, my favorite, is named Jerome (Jerry) Katzoff, six years old. It's a terrible thing to die young. Still, it saves a lot of time. Get it? That wonderful circular bench there all around that elm tree (it should live to be old) is a famous bench named

Sidney Hillman. So you see we got benches. What we do *not* have here, what I am suffering from daily, is not enough first-class books. Plenty of best sellers, but first-class literature? . . . I bet you're surprised. I wrote the manager a letter. "Dear Goldstein," I said. "Dear Goldstein, Are we or are we not the People of the Book? I admit by law we're a little nonsectarian, but by and large we are here living mostly People of the Book. Book means mostly to you Bible, Talmud, etc., probably. To me, and to my generation, idealists all, book means BOOKS. Get me? Goldstein, how about putting a little from Jewish Philanthropies into keeping up the reputation for another fifty years. You could do it single-handed, adding very little to the budget. Wake up, brother, while I still got my wits."

That reminds me, another thing, Faithy. I have to tell you a fact. People's brains, I notice, are disappearing all around me. Every day.

Sit down a minute. It's pressing on me. Last one to go is Eliezer Heligman. One day I'm pointing out to him how the seeds, the regular germinating seeds of Stalinist anti-Semitism, existed not only in clockwork, Russian pogrom mentality, but also in the everyday attitude of even Mensheviks to Zionism. He gives me a big fight, very serious, profound, fundamental. If I weren't so sure I was right, I would have thought I was wrong. A couple of days later I pass him, under this tree resting on this exact bench. I sit down also. He's with Mrs. Grund, a lady well known to be in her second, maybe third, childhood at least.

She's crying. Crying. I don't interfere. Heligman is saying, Madame Grund, you're crying. Why?

My mother died, she says.

Ts, he says.

Died. Died. I was four years old and my mother died.

Ts, he says.

Then my father got me a stepmother.

Oi, says Heligman. It's hard to live with a stepmother. It's terrible. Four years old to lose a mother.

I can't stand it, she says. All day. No one to talk to. She don't care for me, that stepmother. She got her own girl. A girl like me needs a mother.

Oi, says Heligman, a mother, a mother. A girl surely needs a mother.

But not me, I ain't got one. A stepmother I got, no mother.

Oi, says Heligman.

Where will I get a mother from? Never.

Ach, says Heligman. Don't worry, Madame Grund darling, don't worry. Time passes. You'll be healthy, you'll grow up, you'll see. Soon you'll get married, you'll have children, you'll be happy.

Heligman, oi, Heligman, I say, what the hell are you talking about?

Oh, how do you do, he says to me, a passing total stranger. Madame Grund here, he says, is alone in the world, a girl four years old, she lost her mother. (Tears are in his disappearing face.) But I told her she wouldn't cry forever, she'll get married, she'll have children, her time will come, her time will come.

How do you do yourself, Heligman, I say. In fact, goodbye, my dear friend, my best enemy, Heligman, forever goodbye.

Oh Pa! Pa! Faith jumped up. I can't stand your being here.

Really? Who says *I* can stand it?

Then silence.

He picked up a leaf. Here you got it. Gate to Heaven. Ailanthus. They walked in a wide circle in the little garden. They came to another bench: Dedicated to Theodor Herzl Who Saw the Light if Not the Land/In Memory of Mr. and Mrs. Johannes Mayer 1958. They sat close to one another.

Faith put her hand on her father's knee. Papa darling, she said.

Mr. Darwin felt the freedom of committed love. I have to tell the truth. Faith, it's like this. It wasn't on the phone. Ricardo came to visit us. I didn't want to talk in front of the boys. Me and your mother. She was in a state of shock from looking at him. She sent us out for coffee. I never realized he was such an interesting young man.

He's not so young, said Faith. She moved away from her father—but not more than half an inch.

To me he is, said Mr. Darwin. Young. Young is just not old. What's to argue. What you know, *you* know. What I know, *I* know.

Huh! said Faith. Listen, did you know he hasn't come to see the kids. Also, he owes me a chunk of dough.

Aha, money! Maybe he's ashamed. He doesn't have money. He's a man. He's probably ashamed.

Ach, Faith, I'm sorry I told you anything. On the subject of Ricardo, you're demented.

Demented? Boy oh boy, I'm demented. That's nice. You have a kind word from Ricardo and I'm demented.

Calm down, Faithy, please. Can't you lead a more peaceful life? Maybe you call some of this business down on yourself. That's a terrible neighborhood. I wish you'd move.

Move? Where? With what? What are you talking about?

Let's not start that again. I have more to say. Serious things, my dear girl, compared to which Ricardo is a triviality. I have made a certain decision. Your mother isn't in agreement with me. The fact is, I don't want to be in this place anymore. I made up my mind. Your mother likes it. She thinks she's in a nice quiet kibbutz, only luckily Jordan is not on one side and Egypt is not on the other. She sits. She knits. She reads to the blind. She gives a course in what you call needlepoint. She organized the women. They have a history club, Don't Forget the Past. That's the real name, if you can believe it.

Pa, what are you leading up to?

Leading. I'm leading up to the facts of the case. What you said is right. This: I don't want to be here, I told you already. If I don't want to be here, I have to go away. If I go away, I leave Mama. If I leave Mama, well, that's terrible. But, Faith, I can't live here anymore. Impossible. It's not my life. I don't feel old. I never did. I was only sorry for your

mother—we were close companions. She wasn't so
well, to bother with the housework like she used to.
Her operation changed her . . . well, you weren't in
on that trouble. You were already leading your private life . . . well, to her it's like the Grand Hotel
here, only full of *landsmen*. She doesn't see Hegel-
Shtein, a bitter, sour lady. She sees a colorful matri-
arch, full of life. She doesn't see the Bissel twins,
eighty-four years old, tragic, childish, stinking from
urine. She sees wonderful! A whole lifetime together, brothers! She doesn't see, ach! Faithy, she
plain doesn't see!

So?

So Ricardo himself remarked the other day, You
certainly haven't the appearance of an old man, in
and out, up and down the hill, full of ideas.

It's true. . . . Trotsky pointed out, the biggest surprise that comes to a man is old age. O.K. That's
what I mean, I don't feel it. Surprise. Isn't that interesting that he had so much to say on every subject. Years ago I didn't have the right appreciation
of him. Thrown out the front door of history, sneaks
in the window to sit in the living room, excuse me, I
mean I do not feel old. Do NOT. In any respect. You
understand me, Faith?

Faith hoped he didn't really mean what she understood him to mean.

Oh yeah, she said. I guess. You feel active and
healthy. That's what you mean?

Much more, much more. He sighed. How can I
explain it to you, my dear girl. Well, this way. I

have certainly got to get away from here. This is the
end. This is the last station. Right?

Well, right . . .

The last. If it were possible, the way I feel suddenly toward life, I would divorce your mother.

Pa! . . . Faith said. Pa, now you're teasing me.

You, the last person to tease, a person who suffered so much from changes. No. I would divorce
your mother. That would be honest.

Oh, Pa, you wouldn't really, though. I mean you
wouldn't.

I wouldn't leave her in the lurch, of course, but
the main reason—I won't, he said. Faith, you know
why I won't. You must've forgot. Because we were
never married.

Never married?

Never married. I think if you live together so
many years it's almost equally legal as if the rabbi
himself lassoed you together with June roses. Still,
the problem is thorny like the rose itself. If you
never got married, how can you get divorced?

Pa, I've got to get this straight. You are planning
to leave Mama.

No, no, no. I plan to go away from here. If she
comes, good, although life will be different. If she
doesn't, then it must be goodbye.

Never married, Faith repeated to herself. Oh . . .
well, how come?

Don't forget, Faithy, we were a different cut from
you. We were idealists.

Oh, *you* were idealists . . . Faith said. She stood

up, walking around the bench that honored Theodor Herzl. Mr. Darwin watched her. Then she sat down again and filled his innocent ear with the real and ordinary world.

Well, Pa, you know I have three lovers right this minute. I don't know which one I'll choose to finally marry.

What? Faith . . .

Well, Pa, I'm just like you, an idealist. The whole world is getting more idealistic all the time. It's so idealistic. People want only the best, only perfection.

You're making fun.

Fun? What fun? Why did Ricardo get out? It's clear: an idealist. For him somewhere, something perfect existed. So I say, That's right. Me too. Me too. Somewhere for me perfection is flowering. Which of my three lovers do you think I ought to settle for, a high-class idealist like me. *I* don't know.

Faith. Three men, you sleep with three men. I don't believe this.

Sure. In only one week. How about that?

Faithy. Faith. How could you do a thing like that? My God, how? Don't tell your mother. I will never tell her. Never.

Why, what's so terrible, Pa? Just what?

Tell me. He spoke quietly. What for? Why you do such things for them? You have no money, this is it. Yes, he said to himself, the girl has no money.

What are you talking about?

. . . Money.

Oh sure, they pay me all right. How'd you guess?

They pay me with a couple of hours of their valuable time. They tell me their troubles and why they're divorced and separated, and they let me make dinner once in a while. They play ball with the boys in Central Park on Sundays. Oh sure, Pa, I'm paid up to here.

It's not that I have no money, he insisted. You have only to ask me. Faith, every year you are more mixed up than before. What did your mother and me do? We only tried our best.

It sure looks like your best was lousy, said Faith. I want to get the boys. I want to get out of here. I want to get away now.

Distracted, and feeling pains in her jaws, in her right side, in the small infection on her wrist, she ran through the Admitting Parlor, past the library, which was dark, and the busy arts-and-crafts studio. Without a glance, she rushed by magnificent, purple-haired, black-lace-shawled Madame Elena Nazdarova, who sat at the door of the Periodical Department editing the prize-winning institutional journal *A Bessere Zeit*. Madame Nazdarova saw Mr. Darwin, breathless, chasing Faith, and called, Ai, Darwin . . . no love poems this month? How can I go to press?

Don't joke me, don't joke me, Mr. Darwin said, hurrying to catch Faith. Faith, he cried, you go too fast.

So. Oh boy! Faith said, stopping short on the first-floor landing to face him. You're a young man, I thought. You and Ricardo ought to get a nice East

Side pad with a separate entrance so you can entertain separate girls.

Don't judge the world by yourself. Ricardo had his trouble with you. I'm beginning to see the light. Once before I suggested psychiatric help. Charlie is someone with important contacts in the medical profession.

Don't mention Charlie to me. Just don't. I want to get the boys. I want to go now. I want to get out of here.

Don't tell your mother is why I run after you like a fool on the stairs. She had a sister who was also a bum. She'll look at you and she'll know. She'll know.

Don't follow me, Faith yelled.

Lower your voice, Mr. Darwin said between his teeth. Have pride, do you hear me?

Go away, Faith whispered, obedient and frantic. Don't tell your mother.

Shut up! Faith whispered.

The boys are down playing Ping-Pong with Mrs. Reis. She kindly invited them. Faith, what is it? you look black, her mother said.

Breathless, Mr. Darwin gasped, Crazy, crazy like Sylvia, your crazy sister.

Oh her. Mrs. Darwin laughed, but took Faith's hand and pressed it to her cheek. What's the trouble, Faith? Oh yes, you are something like Sylvie. A temper. Oh, she had life to her. My poor Syl, she had zest. She died in front of the television set. She didn't miss a trick.

Oh, Ma, who cares what happened to Sylvie?

What exactly is the matter with you?

A cheerful man's face appeared high in the doorway. Is this the Darwin residence?

Oh, Phil, Faith said. What a time!

What's this? Which one is this? Mr. Darwin shouted.

Philip leaned into the small room. His face was shy and determined, which made him look as though he might leave at any moment. I'm a friend of Faith's, he said. My name is Mazzano. I really came to talk to Mr. Darwin about his work. There are lots of possibilities.

You heard something about me? Mr. Darwin asked. From who?

Faithy, get out the nice china, her mother said.

What? asked Faith.

What do you mean what? What, she repeated, the girl says what.

I'm getting out of here, Faith said. I'm going to get the boys and I'm getting out.

Let her go, Mr. Darwin said.

Philip suddenly noticed her. What shall I do? he asked. What do you want me to do?

Talk to him, I don't care. That's what you want to do. Talk. Right? She thought, This is probably a comedy, this crummy afternoon. Why?

Philip said, Mr. Darwin, your songs are beautiful. Goodbye, said Faith.

Hey, wait a minute, Faith. Please.

No, she said.

. . .

On the beach, the old Brighton Beach of her
childhood, she showed the boys the secret hideout
under the boardwalk, where she had saved the scav-
enged soda-pop bottles. Were they three cents or a
nickel? I can't remember, she said. This was my ter-
ritory. I had to fight for it. But a boy named Eddie
helped me.

Mommy, why do they live there? Do they have
to? Can't they get a real apartment? How come?

I think it's a nice place, said Tonto.

Oh shut up, you jerk, said Richard.

Hey boys, look at the ocean. You know you had
a great-grandfather who lived way up north on the
Baltic Sea, and you know what, he used to skate, for
miles and miles and miles along the shore, with a
frozen herring in his pocket.

Tonto couldn't believe such a fact. He fell over
backwards into the sand. A frozen herring! He
must've been a crazy nut.

Really Ma? said Richard. Did you know him? he
asked.

No, Richie, I didn't. They say he tried to come.
There was no boat. It was too late. That's why I
never laugh at that story Grandpa tells.

Why does Grandpa laugh?

Oh Richie, stop for godsakes.

Tonto, having hit the sand hard, couldn't bear to
get up. He had begun to build a castle. Faith sat
beside him on the cool sand. Richard walked down
to the foamy edge of the water to look past the small

harbor waves, far far out, as far as the sky. Then he came back. His little mouth was tight and his eyes worried. Mom, you have to get them out of there. It's your mother and father. It's your responsibility.

Come on, Richard, they like it. Why is everything my responsibility, every goddamn thing?

It just is, said Richard. Faith looked up and down the beach. She wanted to scream, Help!

Had she been born ten, fifteen years later, she might have done so, screamed and screamed.

Instead, tears made their usual protective lenses for the safe observation of misery.

So bury me, she said, lying flat as a corpse under the October sun.

Tonto immediately began piling sand around her ankles. Stop that! Richard screamed. Just stop that, you stupid jerk. Mom, I was only joking.

Faith sat up. Goddamn it, Richard, what's the matter with you? Everything's such a big deal. I was only joking too. I mean, bury me only up to here, like this, under my arms, you know, so I can give you a good whack every now and then when you're too fresh.

Oh, Ma . . . said Richard, his heart eased in one long sigh. He dropped to his knees beside Tonto, and giving her lots of room for wiggling and whacking, the two boys began to cover most of her with sand.

In the Garden

An elderly lady, wasted and stiff, sat in a garden beside a beautiful young woman whose two children, aged eight and nine, had been kidnapped eight months earlier.

The women were neighbors. They met every afternoon to speak about the children. Their sentences began: When Rosa and Loiza have come home . . . Their sentences often continued: I can't wait to show them the ice-cream freezer Claudina bought us . . . They will probably be afraid to go to school alone. At first Pepi will have to take them in the car . . . They will be thin. No, perhaps they will be too fat, having been forced to eat nothing but rice and beans and pampered with candy and toys to keep them quiet.

The elderly lady thought: When they come home, when they come home . . .

The beautiful young woman, their mother, said,

This pillow cover for Loiza, I don't know if I'll finish it in time. I make so many mistakes, I have to rip. I want it to be perfect.

There were yellow *canario* flowers among green leaves on the pillow slip. There was a hummingbird in each corner.

The two husbands, accompanied by a stranger, came into the garden and waited under the bougainvillea while the father shouted, Coffee! Black! Black! Black! He always shouted these days. His wife retired to the kitchen to make a fourth pot of strong coffee. The father turned to the stranger, speaking as if the visitor were deaf. Now this is a garden, my friend. *This* is beautiful. The life here is good. You can see that. The criminal element is under control at last. The police patrol the area frequently. I can see you're a decent person and I'm glad to have you on this street. We do not rent to Communists or to what you call hippies. Right now in one of my houses the head of the Chicago Medical Center is sleeping. That house across the street there, with the enormous veranda. He sleeps late. It's his vacation from family troubles and business worries. You understand that. We, my colleagues and I, have been responsible for building nearly all the houses you see, the one you've rented. They are well constructed. We want people to come with children and grandchildren. We will not rent to just anyone.

The elderly woman cannot bear his shouting voice. She asks her husband to help her toward home. They slowly move across the lawn.

The stranger sits among the amazing flowers and birds for a few minutes. He is a well-dressed man, middle-aged, who happens to be a Communist. He is also a father of two children who are only a little older than the kidnapped daughters of this household. He is a tenderhearted but relentless person.

In the course of the next few days, as he shops and walks, he speaks to his neighbors, who are friendly. A woman in the corner house often stands at the wrought-iron gate, the *reja*, she calls it, of her veranda. When he asks, Did you know them? she bursts into tears. She says, They never cry anymore, I know. The little one, Loi, played with my granddaughter. When they were tiny, they sat with their dolls right there in the hammock in the back, rocking rocking, little mammies. I thought they would grow up and be friends in life.

He spoke to another neighbor whom he met in a shop. Returning together along the street of palms, the neighbor asked, Did he insult you in any way? No, said the stranger. Well, he often does, you know, some people think he's been driven mad. *I* would be driven mad. I would sell and leave. But he has too much invested here. He hates every one of us.

Why? asked the stranger.

Why not? he replied. Wouldn't you? We are the witnesses of the entire event. Our children are skating up and down the street.

Yes, I see, said the stranger.

A third neighbor was washing his car. (This was another day.) He courteously turned down his car radio, which was singing evangelical songs of salvation. He said, Ah yes, it *is* terrible. Everyone knows, by the way, everyone knows it was his friends who did it. Perhaps he knows too. At least one was deeply involved. We have all been harassed by the police, but I for one am glad to be so pestered. It makes me believe they're doing their work, at least. But one, Carlo—the main one, I think, I'm not afraid to say his name—killed himself under investigation. Just last month. A Cuban. Always laughing.

Was it political? asked the stranger.

No, no, my friend, no politics. Money. Greed. Of course, I'm sure the kidnappers thought: The money will come. What is $100,000 to that person. The children blindfolded a day or so will be returned. No one the wiser. No problem. No one the wiser. They dreamed. A new car—two new cars. An expensive woman in the city. Restaurants. High life. But aha! something went wrong. I'm not afraid to tell you this. *Everyone* knows it. Clearly. The money did not go out quickly enough. Why? Let me tell you why. Because our friend is vain and foolish and believed himself too powerful and lucky to suffer tragic loss. Too quickly (because he is an important man), the police, all, the locals, the federals, moved in. Fear struck the kidnappers, you can see that. You may ask, Where are the children? Perhaps in another country, perhaps kindly treated by a frightened wife. Perhaps they will forget, go to school, they will think—oh, that childhood was a dream. Perhaps they are thrown into the sea. Garbage. Not good, not good.

He turned the radio up. Goodbye, sir, he said.

The very next house belonged to the elderly woman. She sat on the front veranda, a shawl over her knees. Her husband sat beside her. She rolled little metal balls in her hands, an exercise designed to slow the degeneration of her finger muscles.

The stranger stepped up to the *reja* to say goodbye. His vacation was over. He would leave the island in the morning.

Look at this, just look at this, her husband said, waving a newspaper at him. The stranger looked at the article that had been encircled. The reporter had written: "In an interview this afternoon in his summer home in the mountains, Sr. L——, father of the little girls kidnapped almost one year ago, said, Of course they will be returned. If I had less publicity they would have been returned long ago. We expect them home. Their room is ready for them. We believe, my wife and I believe, we are certain they will be returned."

The elderly woman's husband said, What is in his mind? He thinks because he was once a poor boy in a poor country and he became very rich with a beautiful wife, he thinks he can bend steel with his teeth.

The woman spoke slowly. You see, sir, what the world is like. Her face was imperturbable. The wasting disease that deprived her limbs of movement had taken from her the delicate muscular gift of facial expression.

She had been told that this paralysis would soon become much worse. In order to understand that future and practice the little life it would have, she followed the stranger as he departed—without moving her head—with her eyes alone. She watched, from left to right, his gait, his clothes, his hair, his swinging arms. Sadly she had to admit that the eyes' movement even if minutely savored was not such an adventurous journey.

But she had become interested in her own courage.

Somewhere Else

Twenty-two Americans were touring China. I was among them. We took many photographs. We had learned how to say hello, goodbye, may I take your photograph? Frequently the people did not wish to be photographed.

Now, why *is* that? we asked. We take pictures in order to remember the Chinese people better, to be able to tell our friends about them after supper and give slide shows in churches and schools later on. Truthfully, we do it with politics in mind, if not in total command.

Mr. Wong, the political guidance counselor in the Travel Service, said it was because of Antonioni's film on China and his denigrating attraction to archaic charm. His middle-power chauvinism looked on China as the soufflé of Europe, to rise and fall according to the nourishment beaten into it by American capital investment and avant-garde art.

He said the high vigilance of the people would not allow us to imitate this filmmaker's disdain for technologies that visibly assert themselves in urban steel and all along the terraces of rice and soy and wheat.

One day, in the hotel meeting room, he said, You do not love the Chinese people.

Now, he shouldn't have said that. It made us stop listening—especially Ruth Larsen, Ann Reyer, and me. We were to a tourist in love with the Chinese revolution, Mao Tse-tung, and the Chinese people. Those who were affectionate did once in a while hug a guide or interpreter. Others hoped that before the tour ended, they'd be able to walk along a street in Shanghai or Canton holding hands with a Chinese person of their own sex, just as the Chinese did— chatting politics, exchanging ideological news. Surreptitiously we looked into family courtyards every now and then to see real life, from which, though in love, we'd been excluded.

When we began to listen to Mr. Wong again, he was accusing one of us of taking pictures without permission. Where? When? Where? Who? we asked. We hoped we were not about to suffer socialist injustice, because we loved socialism.

Right here in Tientsin, in front of the hotel, Mr. Wong said.

Ah, we thought, it's possible. There were terrible temptations for photograph-taking right across the street from the hotel, in the beautiful small park. There the young played Ping-Pong, the old slowly at 1/25th did Tai Chi. Also, the middle-aged textile workers had left their sewing machines for a few days in order to participate in designing the cloth they fabricated. They stood around the rose garden drawing leaves and roses. One of us could have done that—just snapped a picture, too excited to say, May I please take your photograph?

Mr. Wong continued. The accused, he said, had photographed a lower middle peasant lugging a two-wheel cart full of country produce into the city. A boy had been sleeping on top.

Ah, what a picture! China! The heavy cart, the toiling man, the narrow street—once England's street (huge buildings lined with first-class plumbing for the English empire's waste), like the downtown Free West anywhere. In the foreground the photographed man labored—probably bringing early spring vegetables to some distant neighborhood in order to carry back to his commune honey buckets of the city's stinking gold.

This act, this photographing, had been reported by one vigilant Chinese worker incensed by Antonioni's betrayal. Mr. Wong pointed his political finger at our brilliant comrade Frederick J. Lorenz. You! he said. Especially *you* are not a friend.

A general gasp and three nervous snickers. Immediately Ruth Larsen touched Fred's shoulder to show loyalty. Freddy! Not Freddy! Joe Larsen jumped up. He walked to the door. He put his hand on the knob.

We had all assumed that Mr. Wong's guilty man would be Martin, a jolly friend to all revolutions, an old-time union organizer, history lover, passionate photographer. (Before our tour ended, he had taken

4,387 pictures, although his camera had been broken for two days. It was not exactly broken; it had simply closed its eye, exhausted.)

Ruth, Ann, and I had discussed Freddy. Ruth thought he should have been spoken to long ago, but not for his photography. In this China, where all the grownups dressed in modest gray, blue, and green, Freddy wore very short white California shorts with a mustard-colored California B.V.D. shirt and, above his bronze, blue-eyed face, golden tan California curly hair. She didn't think that was nice.

Who are you, Ruth? The commissar of underwear? Ann had asked.

· At breakfast Ruth had started to address him: Freddy! Then she'd thought, Oh boy! There you go again—the typical analysis by the old, which is: Rough politics is O.K. if it leans on the arm of bourgeois appropriateness. So she'd said, You sure keep your suntan a long time, Freddy.

Fred closed his eyes in order to think in solitude. We suffered a tour-wide two-minute fear. We waited for Fred's decision. He opened his eyes, then rose in high courtroom style to rebut.

Mr. Wong made a little smile. He looked around at us all. His finger pointed once more: You, Mr. Lorenz, have been accused by still another worker of invading a noodle factory.

Cries of No! No! Christ! Come on! He's kidding! Three young people, who liked to see us older folks caught in political contradiction or treasonous bewilderment, simply laughed.

One of us, Duane Smith, had put his life savings

into this trip. He'd studied Chinese for six years in night school in order to come one day to this place and be understood by the Chinese people in Tien An Men Square. He didn't laugh. He whispered, This is serious. What if they throw us out?

Ruth said, Never!

Invading what? said Fred. Joe! he called out. He said, Oh, God! and sat down. What was China talking about?

Joe Larsen chewed sugarless gum very hard. He walked around and around in a little circle of annoyance near the door. Then he moved directly across the room to look at Mr. Wong. He believed in doing that. His politics was based on staring truthfully into the cruel eye of power.

Mr. Wong, he said, you know, in Peking I visited a street noodle factory too. One not far from the hotel.

Joe said he wanted to be absolutely clear. It was his fault that he and Fred had stopped at the noodle shop in the city of Tientsin. He was, when not in China, writing a novel, a utopia, a speculative fiction in which the self-reliant small necessary technology of noodle-making was one short chapter. He had considered it a good omen to have passed this street factory and to have been invited to observe all the soft hanging noodles and, in the bins, the stiff dried noodles. He admired the manageable machine that shaped, cut, and extruded them.

Why is he admitting all that? Duane Smith said. He'll get us thrown out.

Never, said Ruth.

The others had hoped for more interesting admissions. Joe often took long walks when the rest of us were visiting points of cultural interest. At supper he would tell us how he drank tea with old men, a condition he liked to consider himself a member of. He had taken a ferry ride with noisy Chinese families to the other side of a river. There, in an outlying district, two old people—guardians of the street—had shown him how to dispose of a banana peel.

Some of our people with poor character structures were jealous of his adventures. They'd been a little ashamed of their timidity when he spoke, but now that he was being spoken to, they were proud of their group discipline.

Mr. Wong, Joe said, Fred accompanied *me*. He was not alone. It was my idea. I'm crazy about your street noodle factories. Lane factories, I believe you call them?

Mr. Wong looked at Joe. Then he pretended Joe wasn't there and never had been. Mr. Wong did not like to be interfered with right in the middle of a political correction. Also, he did not seem to want to accuse two people at once. Why? Perhaps accusing one person was sharper, required only one finger and one harsh cry. At any rate, he ignored Joe and the interesting socialist question of decentralized neighborhood industry. Instead he said, Mr. Lorenz, why did you choose to photograph that peasant?

What? Me? Me? Me?

Fred said Me? so many times because he was

(and is) one of our foremost movement lawyers. He's accustomed to approbation from his peers and shyness from petitioners. He can be depended upon to take the most hopeless case and to construct, out of his legal education and political experience, hope!—along with a furious protesting constituency.

So once more he cried, Me? Oh, take my film. Take it. Take the camera. You'll see. There's nothing . . . Take it. I don't even *like* to take pictures. I hate the lousy thing.

He tried to jerk the camera off his neck. He failed.

That's true, Mr. Wong, said Martin, trying out a reasonable tone (as one comrade *should* speak to another). My camera was broken last week and he gave me his. It didn't bother him at all.

We are not interested, said Mr. Wong. You will be here twelve more days. We wanted you to know that the Chinese people are vigilant. He made the tiniest bow, turned, and left.

Some of us gathered around Fred. Others gathered as far from Fred as possible.

Later that evening we were invited to share our folk heritage with the Tientsin Women's Federation. We sang "I've Been Working on the Railroad."

The next afternoon Ruth talked to Ho, one of our guides. We all liked him, because he rolled his pants up to the knee when it was hot. She said, You know, Fred's one of our great poor-people's lawyers.

But you guys aren't into law so much, are you? said Ann. She has always been a little sarcastic.

You deserve this, I said to Ho. Who asked you to

invite Antonioni, the star of the declining West? I bet lots of less-known people were dying to make the film.

Let's get off his back, said Martin, composing us nicely in his lens, snapping a group photograph. Duane Smith said, Please! Leave him alone.

Ho had become accustomed to our harassment. He folded his trouser legs one more lap above the knee. But it's right, is it not? he said. You must ask the people first, do they wish to be photographed.

Yes, I said, but that's not the point and you know it, Ho.

And tomorrow, when you visit the countryside and the fisheries, you will inquire before you take a picture of the poor or lower middle peasant?

Sure, said Ann.

You will say, even if it is only a child, may I take your photograph?

O.K., O.K., we said. Relax! We heard you the first five hundred times.

About three months later, Martin invited us to a China reunion at his house, full of food, slides, insights, and commentary. Twelve people came. Ann had flown to Portugal that very morning. Duane Smith had written from California to say naturally he couldn't make it but would Martin lend his fishery slides for a couple of weeks and airmail them at once special delivery, certified. Fred was sure he'd see us; he was due in New York for a week of conferences.

The three young people were present, looking lovely. They were friendly. Two were still solemn with hard new politics, but one who had mocked us with sneers and gloom asked would we please begin the evening by holding hands and singing "Listen, listen, listen to my heart's song, I'll never forget you, I'll never forsake you."

I said, Why not? Let's see what happens.

Ruth said, My God! What's come over you? Anyway, where's Joe?

Someone said we should start either eating or looking. Joe was clearly impossible. He had been undisciplined in two countries. The younger people with the ache of youth were eating all the cheese.

Joe arrived forty minutes late, starved, sweaty. I have to tell you what happened, he said.

You know that nice park in the South Bronx, the one I like, where I've been working on and off this summer? Well, I finished up just a couple of hours ago. The boys I work with had already gone home—we had a great party—and I stuffed the camera and Juan's films of the fiesta into a musette bag.

I knew I was going to see all of you, so I sort of sauntered my way back to the subway, imagining our conversations and, well, excited—you know I get excited.

Those lousy streets. I've been in the neighborhood all these weeks with the summer work kids—not just the park but the lots—building some playgrounds and the kind of giant climber I showed you, Marty. Remember? And filming, getting the kids to see—

not that anyone *sees*. Maybe just to keep a record. Sometimes we're raising a couple of beams and suddenly a building across the street begins to smolder —smoke, big white smoke, then flames out of every window. The Bronx kids usually keep going, but the other boys—they're Puerto Rican too, they come with me from the lower East Side and one boy from Brooklyn—they're amazed. They can't believe—a block tougher than their own. After the fire engines, after the fire, when everything cools off, they like to see the junkies toss brass pipes, real old brass, out of the windows. Some of those houses were nice tenements once.

I know, said Ruth. I lived in one. Me too, said Martin.

That's right. We have some film if you ever want to see—the block is burning down on one side of the street, and the kids are trying to build something on the other.

Anyway, it's such a great day, I just walked along kind of dreaming. I passed a factory. There was a sign, EMPLEADOS NECESITADOS. Took a couple of shots. Women came out of the factory. It was about five-thirty, I guess. They waved, I took some pictures, they waved some more.

Now, you have to understand that on any street there, among a couple dozen abandoned buildings, there's always one or two that look nearly intact. Usually men and boys sit around the front of a building like that. That's what I saw, just a block or two after the factory. I hadn't planned on filming, but we did need a couple of good long background shots—the kids either do that wild back-and-forth panning or they shoot for the eyeball. So I began this slow pan across the top floor—black windows and charred roofs—and as the camera slowly took it all in, I could see out of the corner of my eye a group of guys on one of the stoops. They were a distance away—playing a guitar, leaning on a wall, a mattress, the steps—with a couple of transistors.

I had an awful uncomfortable feeling about including them in the long pan. In fact, I can't remember—did I, or did I stop short? I may have wanted to include them—because I hate those typical exposés, you know. It could have been right—correct—to show that energy those guys sometimes have in the early evening, not just the nodding-out residents of the famous South Bronx.

Still, I know that any non-Hispanic white man with a camera looks like a narc. So I put the camera away. Well, what did I do then? I guess I continued my walk toward the subway—a little quickly, maybe. I knew I'd better move.

About ten seconds after I began to feel safe, I heard a running thud. A human form flew past me, ripping the musette bag off my shoulder. He kept going, swerved, cut across an empty lot to the next street. He was so fast and so violent, but he'd just thrust his arm through the shoulder strap, moving it from my shoulder to his—hadn't hurt me at all, a craftsman—but I was shook up. I stood still. My heart was jumping. I watched him. I turned. Those guys down the block were all laughing. We were the only people on that long burned-out block.

What could I do? I started to resume my lifelong trip to the subway, but I'll tell you I couldn't stand for it to end that way. For some reason I wanted them to know who I was. Also, I didn't want to become scared of walking around that neighborhood. I work there, damn it. I don't know if those are the real reasons. Whatever—I had to talk to them. So I walked back and went up to them. They laughed. I said, Listen, I know it probably wasn't so great to have shot that film over your heads like that, but I don't think I included you.

I told them they probably knew me—I was working a couple of blocks away, and at least a couple of them must have been over there. I said the film I'd shot was not so important, but the other stuff had been taken by the Youth Corps kids and they'd feel bad.

The fellow on the top step said, That's one sad story, old man. I looked up. On the fire escape above us, the guy who'd snatched the musette bag was unraveling the film right out of the camera. Hopping around, dancing, laughing.

That's O.K., I said, like some kind of jerk. I don't really care, but I would like the other film. Can't do it, the guy says. I kept pushing: It isn't mine—it's the kids' on 141st. Then I just stood there looking at them. I didn't move. Couldn't. I must have looked so dumb, or maybe they recognized me. Anyway, they had a small speedy Spanish conference, and the leader, top step man, hollered up, Paco, bring it down. No, no, Paco says. He was draping the exposed film in and out of the fire-escape bars. Bring it down, top-step said. Paco looked absolutely miserable, but he handed the bag over. He was disgusted.

I told them thanks. They said, That's O.K., man. Then I did something strange. Why, I don't know. I said, It's true I need the film, but here, you take the camera.

No, no, said the leader.

Take it, I said.

No, no—you crazy, man?

Listen, take it, use it. We'll come over and help you out. You can make a movie.

Don't want it—you deaf? *No.* No.

I said, You've got to take it. I'll be on the 143rd Street lot.

I shoved the camera into their hands. I walked away fast. And here I am—that's all there is. What do you think?

What in the world! said Ruth.

Forget the world, said Joe. I'm sorry I told you the story. I don't know why I did. I must be nuts.

Martin said, I know why you told the story. You wanted to show that just because a person owns a camera they do not own the whole world and you understand it.

That's what you think, said Joe. I think I told it to you because it just happened. Don't make a big Marxist deal about it.

O.K., don't get upset, said Martin. He began to

fuss with the projector. Now, let's be calm, he said. Get your chairs, everybody. Ruthie, put the lights out. Wait'll you see the color, folks. Number one. Here it comes, that old man, he's holding that grandchild in a pink and orange sweater—where was that?

Oh, Christ, said Joe, can't you remember anything? It was in a courtyard in a village near Nanking.

Lavinia: An Old Story

Lavinia was born laughing. That's how come her disposition so appealing, Robert, how come you in love with her, not Elsie Rose nor Rosemary. Pretty they be, they all come out of me with a grievance. *And* the boys, J. C. Charles and Edward William, from the first second it seem, louder than their sisters. UNcontrollable.

It come from nature, that fact. My opinion: What men got to do on earth don't take more time than sneezing. Now a woman walk away from a man, she just know she loaded down in her body nine months. She got that responsibility on her soul forever.

A man restless all the time owing it to nature to scramble for opportunity. His time took up with nonsense, you know his conversation got to suffer. A man can't talk. That little minute in his mind most the time. Once a while busywork, machinery, cars, guns. Opposite of facts, you got to give in, Robert.

You listen now, boy, Lavinia born in good cheer. Nothing but a crumple sock, a newborn baby, she got a grin acrost her face.

Now, you say you love her. You got three rooms, front, sunny, you want her up there with you. I'm gonna ask you a question. How your job? You a happy worker? Or you dissatisfied, complaining to the boss, upsetting your mother with your dissatisfaction. Ask you another: You ever had welfare? You lie to the relief? I can't see a liar and am against a poor-dispositioned person.

Well, me and Mr. Grimble pull together. He didn't have a dollar, I made do. We live. When he pass away, it be all on me, them devilish boys and them mopey girls.

School, I said to them, you have had it. This here time is Depression. Mr. Roosevelt says so. The green-grocer hisself sitting amids barrels of plenty is skin and bones. Out, I said. You want to learn, learn by night. You spect to eat, work by day.

The big ones took it all right, little ones whine not to have their mama always about. Not Lavinia. Now, Robert, I got to tell you, she so cheerful with foolish stories to tickle the babies. She just rumple up the eldsters. A child, that's all. But I work for folks then, said: Bring that child, she just fine to talk to Granny while you ironing. We don't mind you bring *that* child.

So you see, Robert, when old John Stuart married our Rosemary last week, I said: Take her John Stuart. You and me play Spin the Bottle years and years ago and it some offense you prefer a hankering disarranged girl to a sensible widow that's got some feeling. It's a fact, though, that child does *need* protection. She lack caution. So I gives her to you my old friend, hoping you a better husband to her than you been to poor Mrs. Lucy Stuart gone only seven months.

In fact, who take Elsie is welcome to her. No matter she just sixteen, she never put her mind to nothing large and ain't going to soon.

Tell the truth Robert, it don't seem so far away in my mind, it don't seem distant from this front porch that Grimble first set his eye on me. I was a grade scholar then, aiming high. All in every way I look was on their back providing for men or on their knees cleaning up after them.

I said: Mama, I see you just defile by leaning on every will and whim of Pa's. Now I aim high. To be a teacher and purchase my own grits and not depend on any man.

That was my thought when Mr. Grimble turn to me. He was a smart man, incline to understanding, but his heart been darken by moodiness. Oh my, he liked me.

Now, he was a smart man Robert, but no education. He turn it all to strength till he got shorn by pride. He could heave a meaty hog and that's no lie. In the W.P.A. he was sought for.

I said: Grimble, I just determined not to set myself drifting in this animal way. I just as well live out a spinster's peevish time as be consumed by boiling wash water.

Grimble said: There is ways and means. If you

wish not to have little ones, or just one or two for
comfort, I say yes. I do not want you to pass your
ma's pitiful days. I wish you well.

But you knows men as good as me. When they
warm, they got to cool off. No ways out of that.
Robert, you recollect your own ma, the children that
grown ain't but half. Some discourage in me before
they born, some scotch in my own flesh. And one little baby, crawling off, drown in springtime in that
hole there by the creek.

Grimble tell me, Put that sorrow out of your
mind. It can't be lived with. We got Elsie Rose and
Rosemary and that glad Lavinia. J. C. Charles and
Edward William look so hearty. Preserve yourself.
The Lord says: Endure.

Well, he was sorry to see I never gain my strong
desire to teach. But he provide no help nor no friendship neither, for lean days begun to gnaw into the
fat ones.

Time pass and I sees him clear, but that time I
was rancorous.

I near forgot my reading but that J. C. Charles
was so slow and needed help and that was pleasure
to do. In summer when the light was long, me and
the boy studied. I come close to loving him best, but
he was too slow for my affection.

Then one bad day a man from the quarry come
running. Now listen to me, he say. What Grimble
did. The foreman holler, Now you two hoist that
rock from where it moored. Git it yonder. Well,
listen, we went forward. Then Grimble brag, You
scrawny hod carrier, if'n I can't hoist that pitiful

rock myself, I'm made to swing a broom. No, then the pusher says, no. No, Grimble, that sandstone's got bottom. But him stubborn, gits to it, levers it up, hike his shoulder to it, heaves, and has it sure enough. Then down on his knees using what he got, a goddamn blockhead, and set it just so. Then—now listen—he stand up and turn to look at us. But his face got no appearance. And that Samson sets down and decline to fall but sets like an idiot. Mrs. Grimble, your man's blood vessel is busted.

I only giving you a true idea of life, Robert, for some folk *will* paint it prettier than it truly be.

What I mean about Lavinia—look here at me. Ain't nothing I own but this here apron and that Sunday hat Grimble give me twenty years ago. Now see Lavinia going about improving the foolish, singing in the choir, mending the lame. Now see her, Robert, that gal apt to be a lady preacher, a nurse, something great and have a name. Don't know what you see Robert, but I got in mind to be astonished.

That just what I said to Robert one year just past Christmas. Days still lean and mean. Old Grimble gone, save from misery. Then Robert said to me: How come you set on making me so fearful? You got to know I care for Lavinia. I don't mean no harm to her. Ain't she got her high school? I ain't a bad man. I don't lie. I like her hopeful nature. I like her smart way. Just what you got in mind, Ma?

That was all out of him. Call me Ma and slam the door.

· · ·

Then a long time pass and all growed and gone, but Edward William, a boy concern with nastiness. Then this day come:

Just visiting Lavinia, I see her near scalded, deep in the washtub. Robert Grimble Fenner, Junior, my grandboy, is setting on a stool and squeaking out his schoolday story. Our Lavinia can't stop appreciating him a minute to heed my presence. By my side is Edward William, just wiggling to get away off someplace and start admiring hisself. He is fifteen and my patience is done. So I spurn him to look at that girl. Her little baby, Vynetta, is demanding her and Robert Junior follow her off to the cradle squeaking minus a letup.

I watch that gal. I just stare out my sad-old-sighted eyes at her. What I see: she is busy and broad.

Then I let out a curse, Lord never heard me do in this long life. I cry out loud as my throat was made to do, Damn you, Lavinia—for my heart is busted in a minute—damn you, Lavinia, ain't nothing gonna come of you neither.

Friends

To put us at our ease, to quiet our hearts as she
lay dying, our dear friend Selena said, Life, after
all, has not been an unrelieved horror—you know, I
did have many wonderful years with her.

She pointed to a child who leaned out of a portrait
on the wall—long brown hair, white pinafore, head
and shoulders forward.

Eagerness, said Susan. Ann closed her eyes.

On the same wall three little girls were photographed in a schoolyard. They were in furious discussion; they were holding hands. Right in the
middle of the coffee table, framed, in autumn colors,
a handsome young woman of eighteen sat on an
enormous horse—aloof, disinterested, a rider. One
night this young woman, Selena's child, was found
in a rooming house in a distant city, dead. The police
called. They said, Do you have a daughter named
Abby?

And with *him*, too, our friend Selena said. We had good times, Max and I. You know that.

There were no photographs of *him*. He was married to another woman and had a new, stalwart girl of about six, to whom no harm would ever come, her mother believed.

Our dear Selena had gotten out of bed. Heavily but with a comic dance, she soft-shoed to the bathroom, singing, "Those were the days, my friend . . ."

Later that evening, Ann, Susan, and I were enduring our five-hour train ride to home. After one hour of silence and one hour of coffee and the sandwiches Selena had given us (she actually stood, leaned her big soft excavated body against the kitchen table to make those sandwiches), Ann said, Well, we'll never see *her* again.

Who says? Anyway, listen, said Susan. Think of it. Abby isn't the only kid who died. What about that great guy, remember Bill Dalrymple—he was a non-cooperator or a deserter? And Bob Simon. They were killed in automobile accidents. Matthew, Jeannie, Mike. Remember Al Lurie—he was murdered on Sixth Street—and that little kid Brenda, who O.D.'d on your roof, Ann? The tendency, I suppose, is to forget. You people don't remember them.

What do you mean, "you people"? Ann asked. You're talking to *us*.

I began to apologize for not knowing them all. Most of them were older than my kids, I said.

Of course, the child Abby was exactly in my time of knowing and in all my places of paying attention

—the park, the school, our street. But oh! It's true! Selena's Abby was not the only one of that beloved generation of our children murdered by cars, lost to war, to drugs, to madness.

Selena's main problem, Ann said—you know, she didn't tell the truth.

What?

A few hot human truthful words are powerful enough, Ann thinks, to steam all God's chemical mistakes and society's slimy lies out of her life. We all believe in that power, my friends and I, but sometimes . . . the heat.

Anyway, I always thought Selena had told us a lot. For instance, we knew she was an orphan. There were six, seven other children. She was the youngest. She was forty-two years old before someone informed her that her mother had *not* died in childbirthing her. It was some terrible sickness. And she had lived close to her mother's body—at her breast, in fact—until she was eight months old. Whew! said Selena. What a relief! I'd always felt I was the one who'd killed her.

Your family stinks, we told her. They really held you up for grief.

Oh, people, she said. Forget it. They did a lot of nice things for me too. Me and Abby. Forget it. Who has the time?

That's what I mean, said Ann. Selena should have gone after them with an ax.

More information: Selena's two sisters brought her to a Home. They were ashamed that at sixteen and nineteen they could not take care of her. They kept hugging her. They were sure she'd cry. They took her to her room—not a room, a dormitory with about eight beds. This is your bed, Lena. This is your table for your things. This little drawer is for your toothbrush. All for me? she asked. No one else can use it? Only me. That's all? Artie can't come? Franky can't come? Right?

Believe me, Selena said, those were happy days at Home.

Facts, said Ann, just facts. Not necessarily the *truth*.

I don't think it's right to complain about the character of the dying or start hustling all their motives into the spotlight like that. Isn't it amazing enough, the bravery of that private inclusive intentional community?

It wouldn't help not to be brave, said Selena. You'll see.

She wanted to get back to bed. Susan moved to help her.

Thanks, our Selena said, leaning on another person for the first time in her entire life. The trouble is, when I stand, it hurts me here all down my back. Nothing they can do about it. All the chemotherapy. No more chemistry left in me to therapeut. Ha! Did you know before I came to New York and met you I used to work in that hospital? I was supervisor in gynecology. Nursing. They were my friends, the doctors. They weren't so snotty then. David Clark, big surgeon. He couldn't look at me last week. He kept saying, Lena . . . Lena . . . Like that. We were in North Africa the same year—'44, I think. I told him, Davy, I've been around a long enough time. I haven't missed too much. He knows it. But I didn't want to make him look at me. Ugh, my damn feet are a pain in the neck.

Recent research, said Susan, tells us that it's the neck that's a pain in the feet.

Always something new, said Selena, our dear friend.

On the way back to the bed, she stopped at her desk. There were about twenty snapshots scattered across it—the baby, the child, the young woman. Here, she said to me, take this one. It's a shot of Abby and your Richard in front of the school—third grade? What a day! The show those kids put on! What a bunch of kids! What's Richard doing now?

Oh, who knows? Horsing around someplace. Spain. These days, it's Spain. Who knows where he is? They're all the same.

Why did I say that? I knew exactly where he was. He writes. In fact, he found a broken phone and was able to call every day for a week—mostly to give orders to his brother but also to say, Are you O.K., Ma? How's your new boyfriend, did he smile yet?

The kids, they're all the same, I said.

It was only politeness, I think, not to pour my boy's light, noisy face into that dark afternoon. Richard used to say in his early mean teens, You'd sell us down the river to keep Selena happy and innocent. It's true. Whenever Selena would say, I don't know, Abby has some peculiar friends, I'd answer for stupid comfort, You should see Richard's.

Still, he's in Spain, Selena said. At least you know that. It's probably interesting. He'll learn a lot. Richard is a wonderful boy, Faith. He acts like a wise guy but he's not. You know the night Abby died, when the police called me and told me? That was my first night's sleep in two years. I *knew* where she was.

Selena said this very matter-of-factly—just offering a few informative sentences.

But Ann, listening, said, Oh!—she called out to us all, Oh!—and began to sob. Her straightforwardness had become an arrow and gone right into her own heart.

Then a deep tear-drying breath: I want a picture too, she said.

Yes. Yes, wait, I have one here someplace. Abby and Judy and that Spanish kid Victor. Where is it? Ah. Here!

Three nine-year-old children sat high on that long-armed sycamore in the park, dangling their legs on someone's patient head—smooth dark hair, parted in the middle. Was that head Kitty's?

Our dear friend laughed. Another great day, she said. Wasn't it? I remember you two sizing up the men. I *had* one at the time—I thought. Some joke. Here, take it. I have two copies. But you ought to get it enlarged. When this you see, remember me. Ha-ha. Well, girls—excuse me, I mean ladies—it's time for me to rest.

She took Susan's arm and continued that awful walk to her bed.

We didn't move. We had a long journey ahead of us and had expected a little more comforting before we set off.

No, she said. You'll only miss the express. I'm not in much pain. I've got lots of painkiller. See?

The tabletop was full of little bottles.

I just want to lie down and think of Abby.

It was true, the local could cost us an extra two hours at least. I looked at Ann. It had been hard for her to come at all. Still, we couldn't move. We stood there before Selena in a row. Three old friends. Selena pressed her lips together, ordered her eyes into cold distance.

I know that face. Once, years ago, when the children were children, it had been placed modestly in front of J. Hoffner, the principal of the elementary school.

He'd said, No! Without training you cannot tutor these kids. There are real problems. You have to know *how to teach.*

Our P.T.A. had decided to offer some one-to-one tutorial help for the Spanish kids, who were stuck in crowded classrooms with exhausted teachers among little middle-class achievers. He had said, in a written communication to show seriousness and then in personal confrontation to *prove* seriousness, that he could not allow it. And the board of ed itself had said no. (All this no-ness was to lead to some terrible events in the schools and neighborhoods of our poor

yes-requiring city.) But most of the women in our
P.T.A. were independent—by necessity and disposition. We were, in fact, the soft-speaking tough souls
of anarchy.

I had Fridays off that year. At about 11 a.m. I'd
bypass the principal's office and run up to the fourth
floor. I'd take Robert Figueroa to the end of the hall,
and we'd work away at storytelling for about twenty
minutes. Then we would write the beautiful letters
of the alphabet invented by smart foreigners long
ago to fool time and distance.

That day, Selena and her stubborn face remained
in the office for at least two hours. Finally, Mr.
Hoffner, besieged, said that because she was a nurse,
she would be allowed to help out by taking the littlest children to the modern difficult toilet. Some of
them, he said, had just come from the barbarous
hills beyond Maricao. Selena said O.K., she'd do
that. In the toilet she taught the little girls which
way to wipe, as she had taught her own little girl a
couple of years earlier. At three o'clock she brought
them home for cookies and milk. The children of
that year ate cookies in her kitchen until the end of
the sixth grade.

Now, what did we learn in that year of my Friday
afternoons off? The following: Though the world
cannot be changed by talking to one child at a time,
it may at least be known.

Anyway, Selena placed into our eyes for long
remembrance that useful stubborn face. She said,
No. Listen to me, you people. Please. I don't have

lots of time. What I want . . . I want to lie down and think about Abby. Nothing special. Just think about her, you know.

In the train Susan fell asleep immediately. She woke up from time to time, because the speed of the new wheels and the resistance of the old track gave us some terrible jolts. Once, she opened her eyes wide and said, You know, Ann's right. You don't get sick like that for nothing. I mean, she didn't even mention him.

Why should she? She hasn't even seen him, I said. Susan, you still have him-itis, the dread disease of females.

Yeah? And you don't? Anyway, he *was* around quite a bit. He was there every day, nearly, when the kid died.

Abby. I didn't like to hear "the kid." I wanted to say "Abby" the way I've said "Selena"—so those names can take thickness and strength and fall back into the world with their weight.

Abby, you know, was a wonderful child. She was in Richard's classes every class till high school. Good-hearted little girl from the beginning, noticeably kind—for a kid, I mean. Smart.

That's true, said Ann, very kind. She'd give away Selena's last shirt. Oh yes, they were all wonderful little girls and wonderful little boys.

Chrissy *is* wonderful, Susan said.

She *is*, I said.

Middle kids aren't supposed to be, but she is. She

put herself through college—I didn't have a cent—
and now she has this fellowship. And, you know, she
never did take any crap from boys. She's something.

Ann went swaying up the aisle to the bathroom.
First she said, Oh, all of them—just wohunderful.

I loved Selena, Susan said, but she never talked to
me enough. Maybe she talked to you women more,
about things. Men.

Then Susan fell asleep.

Ann sat down opposite me. She looked straight
into my eyes with a narrow squint. It often connotes
accusation.

Be careful—you're wrecking your laugh lines, I
said.

Screw you, she said. You're kidding around. Do
you realize I don't know where Mickey is? You
know, you've been lucky. You always have been.
Since you were a little kid. Papa and Mama's
darling.

As is usual in conversations, I said a couple of
things out loud and kept a few structured remarks
for interior mulling and righteousness. I thought:
She's never even met my folks. I thought: What a
rotten thing to say. Luck—isn't it something like an
insult?

I said, Annie, I'm only forty-eight. There's lots of
time for me to be totally wrecked—if I live, I mean.

Then I tried to knock wood, but we were sitting in
plush and leaning on plastic. Wood! I shouted.
Please, some wood! Anybody here have a match-
stick?

Oh, shut up, she said. Anyway, death doesn't count.

I tried to think of a couple of sorrows as irreversible as death. But truthfully nothing in my life can compare to hers: a son, a boy of fifteen, who disappears before your very eyes into a darkness or a light behind his own, from which neither hugging nor hitting can bring him. If you shout, Come back, come back, he won't come. Mickey, Mickey, Mickey, we once screamed, as though he were twenty miles away instead of right in front of us in a kitchen chair; but he refused to return. And when he did, twelve hours later, he left immediately for California.

Well, some bad things have happened in my life, I said.

What? You were born a woman? Is that it?

She was, of course, mocking me this time, referring to an old discussion about feminism and Judaism. Actually, on the prism of isms, both of those do have to be looked at together once in a while.

Well, I said, my mother died a couple of years ago and I still feel it. I think *Ma* sometimes and I lose my breath. I miss her. You understand that. Your mother's seventy-six. You have to admit it's nice still having her.

She's very sick, Ann said. Half the time she's out of it.

I decided not to describe my mother's death. I could have done so and made Ann even more miserable. But I thought I'd save that for her next attack on me. These constrictions of her spirit were coming closer and closer together. Probably a great enmity was about to be born.

Susan's eyes opened. The death or dying of someone near or dear often makes people irritable, she stated. (She's been taking a course in relationships *and* interrelationships.) The real name of my seminar is Skills: Personal Friendship and Community. It's a very good course despite your snide remarks.

While we talked, a number of cities passed us, going in the opposite direction. I had tried to look at New London through the dusk of the windows. Now I was missing New Haven. The conductor explained, smiling: Lady, if the windows were clean, half of you'd be dead. The tracks are lined with sharpshooters.

Do you believe that? I hate people to talk that way.

He may be exaggerating, Susan said, but don't wash the window.

A man leaned across the aisle. Ladies, he said, I do believe it. According to what I hear of this part of the country, it don't seem unplausible.

Susan turned to see if he was worth engaging in political dialogue.

You've forgotten Selena already, Ann said. All of us have. Then you'll make this nice memorial service for her and everyone will stand up and say a few words and then we'll forget her again—for good. What'll you say at the memorial, Faith?

It's not right to talk like that. She's not dead yet, Annie.

Yes, she is, said Ann.

We discovered the next day that give or take an hour or two, Ann had been correct. It was a combination—David Clark, surgeon, said—of being sick unto real death and having a tabletop full of little bottles.

Now, why are you taking all those hormones? Susan had asked Selena a couple of years earlier. They were visiting New Orleans. It was Mardi Gras.

Oh, they're mostly vitamins, Selena said. Besides, I want to be young and beautiful. She made a joking pirouette.

Susan said, That's absolutely ridiculous.

But Susan's seven or eight years younger than Selena. What did she know? Because: People *do* want to be young and beautiful. When they meet in the street, male or female, if they're getting older they look at each other's face a little ashamed. It's clear they want to say, Excuse me, I didn't mean to draw attention to mortality and gravity all at once. I didn't want to remind you, my dear friend, of our coming eviction, first from liveliness, then from life. To which, most of the time, the friend's eyes will courteously reply, My dear, it's nothing at all. I hardly noticed.

Luckily, I learned recently how to get out of that deep well of melancholy. Anyone can do it. You grab at roots of the littlest future, sometimes just stubs of conversation. Though some believe you miss a great deal of depth by not sinking down down down.

Susan, I asked, you still seeing Ed Flores?

Went back to his wife.

Lucky she didn't kill you, said Ann. I'd never fool around with a Spanish guy. They all have tough ladies back in the barrio.

No, said Susan, she's unusual. I met her at a meeting. We had an amazing talk. Luisa is a very fine woman. She's one of the office-worker organizers I told you about. She only needs him two more years, she says. Because the kids—they're girls—need to be watched a little in their neighborhood. The neighborhood is definitely not good. He's a good father but not such a great husband.

I'd call that a word to the wise.

Well, you know me—I don't want a husband. I like a male person around. I hate to do without. Anyway, listen to this. She, Luisa, whispers in my ear the other day, she whispers, Suzie, in two years you still want him, I promise you, you got him. Really, I may still want him then. He's only about forty-five now. Still got a lot of spunk. I'll have my degree in two years. Chrissy will be out of the house.

Two years! In two years we'll all be dead, said Ann.

I know she didn't mean all of us. She meant Mickey. That boy of hers would surely be killed in one of the drugstores or whorehouses of Chicago, New Orleans, San Francisco. I'm in a big beautiful city, he said when he called last month. Makes New York look like a garbage tank.

Mickey! Where?

Ha-ha, he said, and hung up.

Soon he'd be picked up for vagrancy, dealing, small thievery, or simply screaming dirty words at night under a citizen's window. Then Ann would fly to the town or not fly to the town to disentangle him, depending on a confluence of financial reality and psychiatric advice.

How *is* Mickey? Selena had said. In fact, that was her first sentence when we came, solemn and embarrassed, into her sunny front room that was full of the light and shadow of windy courtyard trees. We said, each in her own way, How are you feeling, Selena? She said, O.K., first things first. Let's talk about important things. How's Richard? How's Tonto? How's John? How's Chrissy? How's Judy? How's Mickey?

I don't want to talk about Mickey, said Ann.

Oh, let's talk about him, talk about him, Selena said, taking Ann's hand. Let's all think before it's too late. How did it start? Oh, for godsake talk about him.

Susan and I were smart enough to keep our mouths shut.

Nobody knows, nobody knows anything. Why? Where? Everybody has an idea, theories, and writes articles. Nobody knows.

Ann said this sternly. She didn't whine. She wouldn't lean too far into Selena's softness, but listening to Selena speak Mickey's name, she could sit in her chair more easily. I watched. It was interesting. Ann breathed deeply in and out the way we've learned in our Thursday-night yoga class. She was able to rest her body a little bit.

We were riding the rails of the trough called Park-Avenue-in-the-Bronx. Susan had turned from us to talk to the man across the aisle. She was explaining that the war in Vietnam was not yet over and would not be, as far as she was concerned, until we repaired the dikes we'd bombed and paid for some of the hopeless ecological damage. He didn't see it that way. Fifty thousand American lives, our own boys—we'd paid, he said. He asked us if we agreed with Susan. Every word, we said.

You don't look like hippies. He laughed. Then his face changed. As the resident face-reader, I decided he was thinking: Adventure. He may have hit a mother lode of late counterculture in three opinionated left-wing ladies. That was the nice part of his face. The other part was the sly out-of-town-husband-in-New-York look.

I'd like to see you again, he said to Susan.

Oh? Well, come to dinner day after tomorrow. Only two of my kids will be home. You ought to have at least one decent meal in New York.

Kids? His face thought it over. Thanks. Sure, he said. I'll come.

Ann muttered, She's impossible. She did it again.

Oh, Susan's O.K., I said. She's just right in there. Isn't that good?

This is a long ride, said Ann.

Then we were in the darkness that precedes Grand Central.

We're irritable, Susan explained to her new pal.

We're angry with our friend Selena for dying. The reason is, we want her to be present when we're dying. We all require a mother or mother-surrogate to fix our pillows on that final occasion, and we were counting on her to be that person.

I know just what you mean, he said. You'd like to have someone around. A little fuss, maybe.

Something like that. Right, Faith?

It always takes me a minute to slide under the style of her public-address system. I agreed. Yes.

The train stopped hard, in a grinding agony of opposing technologies.

Right. Wrong. Who cares? Ann said. She didn't have to die. She really wrecked everything.

Oh, Annie, I said.

Shut up, will you? Both of you, said Ann, nearly breaking our knees as she jammed past us and out of the train.

Then Susan, like a New York hostess, began to tell that man all our private troubles—the mistake of the World Trade Center, Westway, the decay of the South Bronx, the rage in Williamsburg. She rose with him on the escalator, gabbing into evening friendship and, hopefully, a happy night.

At home Anthony, my youngest son, said, Hello, you just missed Richard. He's in Paris now. He had to call collect.

Collect? From Paris?

He saw my sad face and made one of the herb teas used by his peer group to calm their over-wrought natures. He does want to improve my pretty good health and spirits. His friends have a book that says a person should, if properly nutritioned, live forever. He wants me to give it a try. He also believes that the human race, its brains and good looks, will end in his time.

At about 11:30 he went out to live the pleasures of his eighteen-year-old nighttime life.

At 3 a.m. he found me washing the floors and making little apartment repairs.

More tea, Mom? he asked. He sat down to keep me company. O.K., Faith. I know you feel terrible. But how come Selena never realized about Abby?

Anthony, what the hell do I realize about you?

Come on, you had to be blind. I was just a little kid, and *I* saw. Honest to God, Ma.

Listen, Tonto. Basically Abby was O.K. She was. You don't know yet what their times can do to a person.

Here she goes with her goody-goodies—everything is so groovy wonderful far-out terrific. Next thing, you'll say people are darling and the world is *so* nice and round that Union Carbide will never blow it up.

I have never said anything as hopeful as that. And why to all our knowledge of that sad day did Tonto at 3 a.m. have to add the fact of the world?

The next night Max called from North Carolina. How's Selena? I'm flying up, he said. I have one early-morning appointment. Then I'm canceling everything.

At 7 a.m. Annie called. I had barely brushed my

morning teeth. It was hard, she said. The whole damn thing. I don't mean Selena. All of us. In the train. None of you seemed real to me.

Real? Reality, huh? Listen, how about coming over for breakfast?—I don't have to get going until after nine. I have this neat sourdough rye?

No, she said. Oh Christ, no. No!

I remember Ann's eyes and the hat she wore the day we first looked at each other. Our babies had just stepped howling out of the sandbox on their new walking legs. We picked them up. Over their sandy heads we smiled. I think a bond was sealed then, at least as useful as the vow we'd all sworn with husbands to whom we're no longer married. Hindsight, usually looked down upon, is probably as valuable as foresight, since it does include a few facts.

Meanwhile, Anthony's world—poor, dense, defenseless thing—rolls round and round. Living and dying are fastened to its surface and stuffed into its softer parts.

He was right to call my attention to its suffering and danger. He was right to harass my responsible nature. But I was right to invent for my friends and our children a report on these private deaths and the condition of our lifelong attachments.

At That Time, or
The History of a Joke

At that time most people were willing to donate organs. Abuses were expected. In fact there was a young woman whose uterus was hysterically ripped from her by a passing gynecologist. He was distracted, he said, by the suffering of a childless couple in Fresh Meadows. The young woman said, "It wasn't the pain or the embarrassment, but I think any court would certainly award me the earliest uterine transplant that Dr. Heiliger can obtain."

We are not a heartless people and this was done at the lowest judicial level, no need to appeal to state or federal power.

According to the *Times*, one of the young woman's ovaries rejected the new uterus. The other was perfectly satisfied and did not.

"I feel fine," she said, but almost immediately began to swell, for in the soft red warm interior of her womb, there was already a darling rolled-up fetus. It was unfurled in due time, and lo! it was as black as the night which rests our day-worn eyes.

Then: "Sing!" said Heiliger, the scientist, "for see how the myth of man advances on the back of technological achievement, and behold, without conceiving, a virgin has borne a son." This astonishing and holy news was carried to the eye of field, forest, and industrial park, wherever the media had thrust its wireless thumb. The people celebrated and were relatively joyful and the birth was reenacted on giant screens in theaters and on small screens at home.

Only, on the underside of several cities, certain Jews who had observed and suffered the consequence of other virgin births cried out (weeping) (as usual): "It is not He! It is not He!"

No one knew how to deal with them; they were stubborn and maintained a humorless determination. The authorities took away their shortwave and antennae, their stereo screen TV and their temple videotapes. (People were not incarcerated at that time for such social intransigence. Therefore, neither were they rehabilitated.)

Soon this foolish remnant had nothing left. They had to visit one another or wander from town to town in order to say the most ordinary thing to a friend or relative. They had only their shawls and phylacteries, which were used by women too, for women (by that time) had made their great natural advances and were ministers, seers, rabbis, yogis, priests, etc., in well-known as well as esoteric religions.

In their gossipy communications, they whispered the hidden or omitted fact (which some folks had already noticed): The Child WAS A Girl, and since word of mouth is sound made in the echo of God (in the beginning there was the Word and it was without form but wide), ear to mouth and mouth to ear it soon became the people's knowledge, outwitting the computerized devices to which most sensible people had not said a private word for decades anyway.

Then: "O.K.!" said Dr. Heiliger. "It's perfectly true, but I didn't want to make waves in any water as viscous as the seas of mythology. Yes, it is a girl. A virgin born of a virgin."

Throughout the world, people smiled. By that time, sexism and racism had no public life, though they were still sometimes practiced by adults at home. They were as gladdened by one birth as another. And plans were made to symbolically sew the generations of the daughters one to another by using the holy infant's umbilicus. This was luckily flesh *and* symbol. Therefore beside the cross to which people were accustomed there hung the circle of the navel and the wiggly line of the umbilical cord.

But those particular discontented Jews said again, "Wonderful! So? Another tendency heard from! So it's a girl! Praise to the most Highess! But the fact is, we need another virgin birth like our blessed dead want cupping by ancient holistic practitioners."

And so they continued as female and male, descending and undescending, workers in the muddy basement of history, to which, this very day, the poor return when requiring a cheap but stunning garment for a wedding, birth, or funeral.

Anxiety

The young fathers are waiting outside the school.
What curly heads! Such graceful brown mustaches.
They're sitting on their haunches eating pizza and
exchanging information. They're waiting for the
3 p.m. bell. It's springtime, the season of first looking out the window. I have a window box of green-
house marigolds. The young fathers can be seen
through the ferny leaves.

The bell rings. The children fall out of school,
tumbling through the open door. One of the fathers
sees his child. A small girl. Is she Chinese? A little.
Up u-u-p, he says, and hoists her to his shoulders.
U-u-p, says the second father, and hoists his little
boy. The little boy sits on top of his father's head for
a couple of seconds before sliding to his shoulders.
Very funny, says the father.

They start off down the street, right under and
past my window. The two children are still laugh-

ing. They try to whisper a secret. The fathers haven't finished their conversation. The frailer father is uncomfortable; his little girl wiggles too much.

Stop it this minute, he says.

Oink oink, says the little girl.

What'd you say?

Oink oink, she says.

The young father says What! three times. Then he seizes the child, raises her high above his head, and sets her hard on her feet.

What'd I do so bad, she says, rubbing her ankle.

Just hold my hand, screams the frail and angry father.

I lean far out the window. Stop! Stop! I cry.

The young father turns, shading his eyes, but sees. What? he says. His friend says, Hey? Who's that? He probably thinks I'm a family friend, a teacher maybe.

Who're you? he says.

I move the pots of marigold aside. Then I'm able to lean on my elbow way out into unshadowed visibility. Once, not too long ago, the tenements were speckled with women like me in every third window up to the fifth story, calling the children from play to receive orders and instruction. This memory enables me to say strictly, Young man, I am an older person who feels free because of that to ask questions and give advice.

Oh? he says, laughs with a little embarrassment,

says to his friend, Shoot if you will that old gray head. But he's joking, I know, because he has established himself, legs apart, hands behind his back, his neck arched to see and hear me out.

How old are you? I call. About thirty or so?

Thirty-three.

First I want to say you're about a generation ahead of your father in your attitude and behavior toward your child.

Really? Well? Anything else, ma'am.

Son, I said, leaning another two, three dangerous inches toward him. Son, I must tell you that madmen intend to destroy this beautifully made planet. That the murder of our children by these men has got to become a terror and a sorrow to you, and starting now, it had better interfere with any daily pleasure.

Speech speech, he called.

I waited a minute, but he continued to look up. So, I said, I can tell by your general appearance and loping walk that you agree with me.

I do, he said, winking at his friend; but turning a serious face to mine, he said again, Yes, yes, I do.

Well then, why did you become so angry at that little girl whose future is like a film which suddenly cuts to white. Why did you nearly slam this little doomed person to the ground in your uncontrollable anger.

Let's not go too far, said the young father. She *was* jumping around on my poor back and hollering oink oink.

When were you angriest—when she wiggled and jumped or when she said oink?

He scratched his wonderful head of dark well-cut hair. I guess when she said oink.

Have you ever said oink oink? Think carefully. Years ago, perhaps?

No. Well maybe. Maybe.

Whom did you refer to in this way?

He laughed. He called to his friend, Hey Ken, this old person's got something. The cops. In a demonstration. Oink oink, he said, remembering, laughing.

The little girl smiled and said, Oink oink.

Shut up, he said.

What do you deduce from this?

That I was angry at Rosie because she was dealing with me as though I was a figure of authority, and it's not my thing, never has been, never will be.

I could see his happiness, his nice grin, as he remembered this.

So, I continued, since those children are such lovely examples of what may well be the last generation of humankind, why don't you start all over again, right from the school door, as though none of this had ever happened.

Thank you, said the young father. Thank you. It would be nice to be a horse, he said, grabbing little Rosie's hand. Come on Rosie, let's go. I don't have all day.

U-up, says the first father. U-up, says the second.

Giddap, shout the children, and the fathers yell neigh neigh, as horses do. The children kick their fathers' horsechests, screaming giddap giddap, and they gallop wildly westward.

I lean way out to cry once more, Be careful! Stop! But they've gone too far. Oh, anyone would love to be a fierce fast horse carrying a beloved beautiful rider, but they are galloping toward one of the most dangerous street corners in the world. And they may live beyond that trisection across other dangerous avenues.

So I must shut the window after patting the April-cooled marigolds with their rusty smell of summer. Then I sit in the nice light and wonder how to make sure that they gallop safely home through the airy scary dreams of scientists and the bulky dreams of automakers. I wish I could see just how they sit down at their kitchen tables for a healthy snack (orange juice or milk and cookies) before going out into the new spring afternoon to play.

In This Country,
But in Another Language,
My Aunt Refuses to Marry
the Men Everyone
Wants Her To

My grandmother sat in her chair. She said, When I lie down at night I can't rest, my bones push each other. When I wake up in the morning I say to myself, What? Did I sleep? My God, I'm still here. I'll be in this world forever.

My aunt was making the bed. Look, your grandmother, she doesn't sweat. Nothing has to be washed —her stockings, her underwear, the sheets. From this you wouldn't believe what a life she had. It wasn't life. It was torture.

Doesn't she love us? I asked.

Love you? my aunt said. What else is worth it? You children. Your cousin in Connecticut.

So. Doesn't that make her happy?

My aunt said, Ach, what she saw!

What? I asked. What did she see?

Someday I'll tell you. One thing I'll tell you right now. Don't carry the main flag. When you're bigger, you'll be in a demonstration or a strike or something. It doesn't have to be you, let someone else.

Because Russya carried the flag, that's why? I asked.

Because he was a wonderful boy, only seventeen. All by herself, your grandmother picked him up from the street—he was dead—she took him home in the wagon.

What else? I asked.

My father walked into the room. He said, At least *she* lived.

Didn't you live too? I asked my aunt.

Then my grandmother took her hand. Sonia. One reason I don't close my eyes at night is I think about you. You know it. What will be? You have no life.

Grandmother, I asked, what about us?

My aunt sighed. Little girl. Darling, let's take a nice walk.

At the supper table nobody spoke. So I asked her once more: Sonia, tell me no or yes. Do you have a life?

Ha! she said. If you really want to know, read Dostoevsky. Then they all laughed and laughed.

My mother brought tea and preserves.

My grandmother said to all our faces, Why do you laugh?

But my aunt said, Laugh!

Mother

One day I was listening to the AM radio. I heard a song: "Oh, I Long to See My Mother in the Doorway." By God! I said, I understand that song. I have often longed to see my mother in the doorway. As a matter of fact, she did stand frequently in various doorways looking at me. She stood one day, just so, at the front door, the darkness of the hallway behind her. It was New Year's Day. She said sadly, If you come home at 4 a.m. when you're seventeen, what time will you come home when you're twenty? She asked this question without humor or meanness. She had begun her worried preparations for death. She would not be present, she thought, when I was twenty. So she wondered.

Another time she stood in the doorway of my room. I had just issued a political manifesto attacking the family's position on the Soviet Union. She said, Go to sleep for godsakes, you damn fool, you and your Communist ideas. We saw them already, Papa and me, in 1905. We guessed it all.

At the door of the kitchen she said, You never finish your lunch. You run around senselessly. What will become of you?

Then she died.

Naturally for the rest of my life I longed to see her, not only in doorways, in a great number of places—in the dining room with my aunts, at the window looking up and down the block, in the country garden among zinnias and marigolds, in the living room with my father.

They sat in comfortable leather chairs. They were listening to Mozart. They looked at one another amazed. It seemed to them that they'd just come over on the boat. They'd just learned the first English words. It seemed to them that he had just proudly handed in a 100 percent correct exam to the American anatomy professor. It seemed as though she'd just quit the shop for the kitchen.

I wish I could see her in the doorway of the living room.

She stood there a minute. Then she sat beside him. They owned an expensive record player. They were listening to Bach. She said to him, Talk to me a little. We don't talk so much anymore.

I'm tired, he said. Can't you see? I saw maybe thirty people today. All sick, all talk talk talk talk. Listen to the music, he said. I believe you once had perfect pitch. I'm tired, he said.

Then she died.

Ruthy and Edie

One day in the Bronx two small girls named Edie and Ruthy were sitting on the stoop steps. They were talking about the real world of boys. Because of this, they kept their skirts pulled tight around their knees. A gang of boys who lived across the street spent at least one hour of every Saturday afternoon pulling up girls' dresses. They needed to see the color of a girl's underpants in order to scream outside the candy store, Edie wears pink panties.

Ruthy said, anyway, she liked to play with those boys. They did more things. Edie said she hated to play with them. They hit and picked up her skirt. Ruthy agreed. It *was* wrong of them to do this. But, she said, they ran around the block a lot, had races, and played war on the corner. Edie said it wasn't *that* good.

Ruthy said, Another thing, Edie, you could be a soldier if you're a boy.

So? What's so good about that?

Well, you could fight for your country.

Edie said, I don't want to.

What? Edie! Ruthy was a big reader and most interesting reading was about bravery—for instance Roland's Horn at Roncevaux. Her father had been brave and there was often a lot of discussion about this at suppertime. In fact, he sometimes modestly said, Yes, I suppose I was brave in those days. And so was your mother, he added. Then Ruthy's mother put his boiled egg in front of him where he could see it. Reading about Roland, Ruthy learned that if a country wanted to last, it would require a great deal of bravery. She nearly cried with pity when she thought of Edie and the United States of America.

You don't want to? she asked.

No.

Why, Edie, why?

I don't feel like.

Why, Edie? How come?

You always start hollering if I don't do what you tell me. I don't always have to say what you tell me. I can say whatever I like.

Yeah, but if you love your country you have to go fight for it. How come you don't want to? Even if you get killed, it's worth it.

Edie said, I don't want to leave my mother.

Your mother? You must be a baby. Your mother?

Edie pulled her skirt very tight over her knees. I don't like it when I don't see her a long time. Like when she went to Springfield to my uncle. I don't like it.

Oh boy! said Ruthy. Oh boy! What a baby! She stood up. She wanted to go away. She just wanted to jump from the top step, run down to the corner, and wrestle with someone. She said, You know, Edie, this is *my* stoop.

Edie didn't budge. She leaned her chin on her knees and felt sad. She was a big reader too, but she liked *The Bobbsey Twins* or *Honey Bunch at the Seashore.* She loved that nice family life. She tried to live it in the three rooms on the fourth floor. Sometimes she called her father Dad, or even Father, which surprised him. Who? he asked.

I have to go home now, she said. My cousin Alfred's coming. She looked to see if Ruthy was still mad. Suddenly she saw a dog. Ruthy, she said, getting to her feet. There's a dog coming. Ruthy turned. There *was* a dog about three-quarters of the way down the block between the candy store and the grocer's. It was an ordinary middle-sized dog. But it *was* coming. It didn't stop to sniff at curbs or pee on the house fronts. It just trotted steadily along the middle of the sidewalk.

Ruthy watched him. Her heart began to thump and take up too much space inside her ribs. She thought speedily, Oh, a dog has teeth! It's large, hairy, strange. Nobody can say what a dog is thinking. A dog is an animal. You could talk to a dog, but a dog couldn't talk to you. If you said to a dog, STOP! a dog would just keep going. If it's angry and bites you, you might get rabies. It will take you about six weeks to die and you will die screaming in agony. Your stomach will turn into a rock and you will have lockjaw. When they find you, your mouth will be paralyzed wide open in your dying scream.

Ruthy said, I'm going right now. She turned as though she'd been directed by some far-off switch. She pushed the hall door open and got safely inside. With one hand she pressed the apartment bell. With the other she held the door shut. She leaned against the glass door as Edie started to bang on it. Let me in, Ruthy, let me in, please. Oh, Ruthy!

I can't. Please, Edie, I just can't.

Edie's eyes rolled fearfully toward the walking dog. It's coming. Oh, Ruthy, please, please.

No! No! said Ruthy.

The dog stopped right in front of the stoop to hear the screaming and banging. Edie's heart stopped too. But in a minute he decided to go on. He passed. He continued his easy steady pace.

When Ruthy's big sister came down to call them for lunch, the two girls were crying. They were hugging each other and their hair was a mess. You two are nuts, she said. If I was Mama, I wouldn't let you play together so much every single day. I mean it.

Many years later in Manhattan it was Ruthy's fiftieth birthday. She had invited three friends.

They waited for her at the round kitchen table. She had been constructing several pies so that this birthday could be celebrated in her kitchen during the day by any gathered group without too much trouble. Now and then one of the friends would say, Will you sit down, for godsakes! She would sit immediately. But in the middle of someone's sentence or even one of her own, she'd jump up with a look of worry beyond household affairs to wash a cooking utensil or wipe crumbs of flour off the Formica counter.

Edie was one of the women at the table. She was sewing, by neat hand, a new zipper into an old dress. She said, Ruthy, it wasn't like that. We both ran in and out a lot.

No, said Ruth. You would never have locked me out. You were an awful sissy, sweetie, but you would never, never have locked me out. Just look at yourself. Look at your life!

Edie glanced, as people will, when told to do that. She saw a chubby dark-haired woman who looked like a nice short teacher, someone who stood at the front of the schoolroom and said, History is a wonderful subject. It's all stories. It's where we come from, who we are. For instance, where do you come from, Juan? Where do your parents and grandparents come from?

You know that, Mizz Seiden. Porto Rico. You know that a long-o time-o, Juan said, probably in order to mock both languages. Edie thought, Oh, to whom would he speak?

For Christsakes, this is a party, isn't it? said Ann.
She was patting a couple of small cases and a projector on the floor next to her chair. Was she about
to offer a slide show? No, she had already been pre-
vented from doing this by Faith, who'd looked at
the clock two or three times and said, I don't have the
time, Jack is coming tonight. Ruth had looked at the
clock too. Next week, Ann? Ann said O.K. O.K. But
Ruthy, I want to say you have to quit knocking
yourself. I've seen you do a million good things. If
you were such a dud, why'd I write it down in my
will that if anything happened to me, you and Joe
were the ones who'd raise my kids.

You were just plain wrong. I couldn't even raise
my own right.

Ruthy, really, they're pretty much raised. Anyway, how can you say an awful thing like that?
Edie asked. They're wonderful beautiful brilliant
girls. Edie knew this because she had held them in
her arms the third or fourth day of life. Naturally,
she became the friend called aunt.

That's true, I don't have to worry about Sara anymore, I guess.

Why? Because she's a married mommy? Faith
asked. What an insult to Edie!

No, that's O.K., said Edie.

Well, I do worry about Rachel. I just can't help
myself. I never know where she is. She was supposed
to be here last night. She does usually call. Where
the hell is she?

Oh, probably in jail for some stupid little sit-in or

something, Ann said. She'll get out in five minutes. Why she thinks that kind of thing works is a mystery to me. You brought her up like that and now you're surprised. Besides which, I don't want to talk about the goddamn kids, said Ann. Here I've gone around half of most of the nearly socialist world and nobody asks me a single question. I have been a witness of events! she shouted.

I do want to hear everything, said Ruth. Then she changed her mind. Well, I don't mean everything. Just say one good thing and one bad thing about every place you've been. We only have a couple of hours. (It was four o'clock. At six, Sara and Tomas with Letty, the first grandchild, standing between them would be at the door. Letty would probably think it was her own birthday party. Someone would say, What curly hair! They would all love her new shoes and her newest sentence, which was Remember dat? Because for such a long time there had been only the present full of milk and looking. Then one day, trying to dream into an afternoon nap, she sat up and said, Gramma, I boke your cup. Remember dat? In this simple way the lifelong past is invented, which, as we know, thickens the present and gives all kinds of advice to the future.) So, Ann, I mean just a couple of things about each country.

That's not much of a discussion, for Christsake.

It's a party, Ann, you said it yourself.

Well, change your face, then.

Oh. Ruth touched her mouth, the corners of her eyes. You're right. Birthday! she said.

Well, let's go, then, said Ann. She stated two good things and one bad thing about Chile (an earlier visit), Rhodesia, the Soviet Union, and Portugal.

You forgot about China. Why don't you tell them about our trip to China?

I don't think I will, Ruthy; you'd only contradict every word I say.

Edie, the oldest friend, stripped a nice freckled banana she'd been watching during Ann's talk. The thing is, Ruth, you never simply say yes. I've told you so many times, *I* would have slammed the door on you, admit it, but it was your house, and that slowed me down.

Property, Ann said. Even among poor people, it begins early.

Poor? asked Edie. It was the Depression.

Two questions—Faith believed she'd listened patiently long enough. I love that story, but I've heard it before. Whenever you're down in the dumps, Ruthy. Right?

I haven't, Ann said. How come, Ruthy? Also, will you please sit with us.

The second question: What about this city? I mean, I'm kind of sick of these big international reports. Look at this place, looks like a toxic waste dump. A war. Nine million people.

Oh, that's true, Edie said, but Faith, the whole thing *is* hopeless. Top to bottom, the streets, those kids, dumped, plain dumped. That's the correct word, "dumped." She began to cry.

Cut it out, Ann shouted. No tears, Edie! No! Stop

this minute! I swear, Faith said, you'd better stop that! (They were all, even Edie, ideologically, spiritually, and on puritanical principle against despair.)

Faith was sorry to have mentioned the city in Edie's presence. If you said the word "city" to Edie, or even the cool adjective "municipal," specific children usually sitting at the back of the room appeared before her eyes and refused to answer when she called on them. So Faith said, O.K. New subject: What do you women think of the grand juries they're calling up all over the place?

All over what place? Edie asked. Oh, Faith, forget it, they're going through something. You know you three lead such adversarial lives. I hate it. What good does it do? Anyway, those juries will pass.

Edie, sometimes I think you're half asleep. You know that woman in New Haven who was called? I know her personally. She wouldn't say a word. She's in jail. They're not kidding.

I'd never open my mouth either, said Ann. Never. She clamped her mouth shut then and there.

I believe you, Ann. But sometimes, Ruth said, I think, Suppose I was in Argentina and they had my kid. God, if they had our Sara's Letty, I'd maybe say anything.

Oh, Ruth, you've held up pretty well, once or twice, Faith said.

Yes, Ann said, in fact we were all pretty good that day, we were sitting right up against the horses' knees at the draft board—were you there, Edie? And then the goddamn horses started to rear and the cops were knocking people on their backs and heads—remember? And, Ruthy, I was watching you. You just suddenly plowed in and out of those monsters. You should have been trampled to death. And you grabbed the captain by his gold buttons and you hollered, You bastard! Get your goddamn cavalry out of here. You shook him and shook him.

He ordered them, Ruth said. She set one of her birthday cakes, which was an apple plum pie, on the table. I saw him. He was the responsible person. I saw the whole damn operation. I'd begun to run—the horses—but I turned because I was the one supposed to be in front and I saw him give the order. I've never honestly been so angry.

Ann smiled. Anger, she said. That's really good.

You think so? Ruth asked. You sure?

Buzz off, said Ann.

Ruth lit the candles. Come on, Ann, we've got to blow this out together. And make a wish. I don't have the wind I used to have.

But you're still full of hot air, Edie said. And kissed her hard. What did you wish, Ruthy? she asked.

Well, a wish, some wish, Ruth said. Well, I wished that this world wouldn't end. This world, this world, Ruth said softly.

Me too, I wished exactly the same. Taking action, Ann hoisted herself up onto a kitchen chair, saying, ugh my back, ouch my knee. Then: Let us go forth with fear and courage and rage to save the world.

Bravo, Edie said softly.

Wait a minute, said Faith . . .

Ann said, Oh, you . . . you . . .

But it was six o'clock and the doorbell rang. Sara and Tomas stood on either side of Letty, who was hopping or wiggling with excitement, hiding behind her mother's long skirt or grabbing her father's thigh. The door had barely opened when Letty jumped forward to hug Ruth's knees. I'm gonna sleep in your house, Gramma.

I know, darling, I know.

Gramma, I slept in your bed with you. Remember dat?

Oh sure, darling, I remember. We woke up around five and it was still dark and I looked at you and you looked at me and you had a great big Letty smile and we just burst out laughing and you laughed and I laughed.

I remember dat, Gramma. Letty looked at her parents with shyness and pride. She was still happy to have found the word "remember," which could name so many pictures in her head.

And then we went right back to sleep, Ruth said, kneeling now to Letty's height to kiss her little face.

Where's my Aunt Rachel? Letty asked, hunting among the crowd of unfamiliar legs in the hallway.

I don't know.

She's supposed to be here, Letty said. Mommy, you promised. She's really supposed.

Yes, said Ruth, picking Letty up to hug her and then hug her again. Letty, she said as lightly as she could, She *is* supposed to be here. But where can she be? She certainly is supposed.

Letty began to squirm out of Ruth's arms. Mommy, she called, Gramma is squeezing. But it seemed to Ruth that she'd better hold her even closer, because, though no one else seemed to notice —Letty, rosy and soft-cheeked as ever, was falling, already falling, falling out of her brand-new hammock of world-inventing words onto the hard floor of man-made time.

A Man Told Me
the Story of His Life

Vicente said: I wanted to be a doctor. I wanted to be a doctor with my whole heart.

I learned every bone, every organ in the body. What is it for? Why does it work?

The school said to me: Vicente, be an engineer. That would be good. You understand mathematics.

I said to the school: I want to be a doctor. I already know how the organs connect. When something goes wrong, I'll understand how to make repairs.

The school said: Vicente, you will really be an excellent engineer. You show on all the tests what a good engineer you will be. It doesn't show whether you'll be a good doctor.

I said: Oh, I long to be a doctor. I nearly cried. I was seventeen. I said: But perhaps you're right. You're the teacher. You're the principal. I know I'm young.

The school said: And besides, you're going into the army.

And then I was made a cook. I prepared food for two thousand men.

Now you see me. I have a good job. I have three children. This is my wife, Consuela. Did you know I saved her life?

Look, she suffered pain. The doctor said: What is this? Are you tired? Have you had too much company? How many children? Rest overnight, then tomorrow we'll make tests.

The next morning I called the doctor. I said: She must be operated immediately. I have looked in the book. I see where her pain is. I understand what the pressure is, where it comes from. I see clearly the organ that is making trouble.

The doctor made a test. He said: She must be operated at once. He said to me: Vicente, how did you know?

The Story Hearer

I am trying to curb my cultivated individualism, which seemed for years so sweet. It was my own song in my own world and, of course, it may not be useful in the hard time to come. So, when Jack said at dinner, What did you do today with your year off? I decided to make an immediate public accounting of the day, not to water my brains with time spent in order to grow smart private thoughts.

I said, Shall we begin at the beginning?

Yes, he said, I've always loved beginnings.

Men do, I replied. No one knows if they will ever get over this. Hundreds of thousands of words have been written, some freelance and some commissioned. Still no one knows.

Look here, he said, I like middles too.

Oh yes, I know. I questioned him. Is this due to age or the recent proliferation of newspaper articles?

I don't know, he said. I often wonder, but it seems to me that my father, who was a decent man—your typical nine-to-fiver—it seems to me he settled into a great appreciation of the middle just about the time my mother said, Well, Willy, it's enough. Goodbye. Keep the children warm and let him (me) finish high school at least. Then she kissed him, kissed us kids. She said, I'll call you next week, but never did speak to any of us again. Where can she be?

Now, I've heard that story maybe thirty times and I still can't bear it. In fact, whenever I've made some strong adversary point in public, Jack tells it to grieve me. Sometimes I begin to cry. Sometimes I just make soup immediately. Once I thought, Oh, I'll iron his underwear. I've heard of that being done, but I couldn't find the cord. I haven't needed to iron in years because of famous American science, which gives us wash-and-wear in one test tube and nerve gas in the other. Its right test tube doesn't know what its left test tube is doing.

Oh yes, it does, says Jack.

Therefore I want to go on with the story. Or perhaps begin it again. Jack said, What did you do today with your year off? I said, My dear, in the late morning I left our apartment. The *Times* was folded on the doormat of 1-A. I could see that it was black with earthquake, war, and private murder. Clearly death had been successful everywhere but not—I saw when I stepped out the front door—on our own block. Here it was springtime, partly because of the time of the year and partly because we have a self-involved block-centered street association which has lined us with sycamores and enhanced us with a mountain ash, two ginkgoes, and here and there (because we are part of the whole) ailanthus, city saver.

I said to myself, What a day! I think I'll run down to the store and pick up some comestibles. I actually thought that. Had I simply gone to the store without thinking, the word "comestible" would never have occurred to me. I would have imagined—hungry supper nighttime Jack greens cheese store walk street.

But I do like this language—wheat and chaff—with its widening pool of foreign genes, and since I never have had any occasion to say "comestible," it was pleasurable to think it.

At the grocer's I met an old friend who had continued his life as it had begun—in the avant-garde, but not selfishly. He had also organized guerrilla theater demonstrations and had never spoken ill of the people. Most artists do because they have very small audiences and are angry at those audiences for not enlarging themselves.

How can they do that? I've often asked. They have word of mouth, don't they? most artists peevishly will reply.

Well, first my friend and I talked of the lettuce boycott. It was an old boycott. I told my friend (whose name was Jim) all about the silk-stocking boycott which coincided with the Japanese devastation of Manchuria and the disappearance of the Sixth Avenue El into Japanese factory furnaces to be returned a few years later—sometimes to the very same neighborhood—as shrapnel stuck in the bodies of some young New Yorkers of my generation.

Did that lead to Pearl Harbor? he asked respectfully. He was aware that I had witnessing information of events that had occurred when he was in grade school. That respect gave me all the advantage I needed to be aggressive and critical. I said, Jim, I have been wanting to tell you that I do not believe in the effectiveness of the way that you had the Vietnamese screaming at our last demonstration. I don't think the meaning of our struggle has anything to do with all that racket.

You don't understand Artaud, he said. I believe that the theater is the handmaiden of the revolution.

The valet, you mean.

He deferred to my correction by nodding his head. He accepts criticism gracefully, since he can always meet it with a smiling bumper of iron opinion.

You ought to know more about Artaud, he said.

You're right. I should. But I've been awfully busy. Also, I may have once known a great deal about him. In the last few years, all the characters of literature run together in my head. Sometimes King Ubu appears right next to Mr. Sparsit—or Mrs. . . .

At this point the butcher said, What'll you have, young lady?

I refused to tell him.

Jack, to whom, if you remember, I was telling this daylong story, muttered, Oh God, no! You didn't do that again.

I did, I said. It's an insult. You do not say to a

woman of my age who looks my age, What'll you have, young lady? I did not answer him. If you say that to someone like me, it really means, What do you want, you pathetic old hag?

Are you getting like that now too? he asked.

Look, Jack, I said, face facts. Let's say the butcher meant no harm. Eddie, he's not so bad. He spends two hours coming to New York from Jersey. Then he spends two hours going back. I'm sorry for his long journey. But I still mean it. He mustn't say it anymore.

Eddie, I said, don't talk like that or I won't tell you what I want.

Whatever you say, honey, but what'll you have?

Well, could you cut me up a couple of fryers?

Sure I will, he said.

I'll have a pork butt, said Jim. By the way, you know we're doing a show at City College this summer. Not in the auditorium—in the biology lab. It's a new idea. We had to fight for it. It's the most political thing we've done since *Scavenging*.

Did I hear you say City College? asked Eddie as he cut the little chicken's leg out of its socket. Well, when I was a boy, a kid—what we called City College—you know it was C.C.N.Y. then, well, we called it Circumcised Citizens of New York.

Really, said Jim. He looked at me. Did I object? Was I offended?

The fact of male circumcision doesn't insult me, I said. However, I understand that the clipping of clitorises of young girls continues in Morocco to this day.

Jim has a shy side. He took his pork butt and said goodbye.

I had begun to examine the chicken livers. Sometimes they are tanner than red, but I understand this is not too bad.

Suddenly Treadwell Thomas appeared at my side and embraced me. He's a famous fussy gourmet, and I was glad that the butcher saw our affectionate hug. Thought up any good euphemisms lately? I asked.

Ha ha, he said. He still feels bad about his life in the Language Division of the Defense Department. A year or two ago Jack interviewed him for a magazine called *The Social Ordure*, which ran five quarterly issues before the first editor was hired away by the *Times*. It's still a fine periodical.

Here's part of the interview:

Mr. Thomas, what is the purpose of the Language Division?

Well, Jack, it was organized to discontinue the English language as a useful way to communicate exact facts. Of course, it's not the first (or last) organization to have attempted this, but it's had some success.

Mr. Thomas, is this an ironic statement made in the afterglow of your new idealism and the broad range of classified information it has made available to us?

Not at all, Jack. It wasn't I who invented the expression "protective reaction." And it was Eisenhower, not I, who thought up (while thousands of hydrogen bombs were being tucked into silos and submarines)—it was not I who invented "Atoms for Peace" and its code name, "Operation Wheaties."

Could you give us at least one expression you invented to stultify or mitigate? (Jack, I screamed, "stultify" or "mitigate," you caught the disease. Shut up, said Jack, and returned to the interview.)

Well? he asked.

Well, said Treadwell Thomas, I was asked to develop a word or series of words that could describe, denote any of the Latin American countries in a condition of change—something that would by its mere utterance neutralize or mock their revolutionary situation. After consultation, brainpicking, and the daydreaming that is appropriate to any act of creation, I came up with "revostate." The word was slipped into conversations in Washington; one or two journalists were glad to use it. It was just lingo for a long time. But you have no doubt seen the monograph *The Revostationary Peasant in Brazil Today*. Even you pinkos use it. Not to mention Wasserman's poetic article, "Rain Forest, Still Water, and the Culture of the Revostate," which was actually featured in this journal.

Right on, Treadwell—as our black brothers joyfully said for a couple of years before handing that utterance on for our stultification or mitigation.

Still, it's true Thomas could have gone as far as far happens to be in our time and generation, hundreds of ambitious jobless college students at the foot of his tongue on Senior Defense Department Recruiting Day, but apart from cooking a lot of fish he has chosen to guffaw quite often. Some people

around here think that guffawing, the energetic
cleansing of the nasal passage, is the basic wisdom
of the East. Other people think that's not true.

Which reminded me as we waited for the packag-
ing of the meat, how's Gussie?

Gus? Oh yeah, she's into hydroponics. She's got
all this stuff standing around in tubs. We may never
have to go shopping again.

Well, I laughed and laughed. I repeated the story
to several others before the day was over. I mocked
Gussie to Jack. I spoke of her mockingly to one or
two strangers. And the fact is, she was already the
wave of the future. I was ignorant. It wasn't my
ocean she was a wave in.

In fact, I am stuck here among my own ripples
and tides. Don't you wish you could rise powerfully
above your time and name? I'm sure we all try, but
here we are, always slipping and falling down into
them, speaking their narrow language, though the
subject, which is how to save the world—and quickly
—is immense.

Goodbye, Treadwell, I said sadly. I've got to get
some greens.

The owner of our grocery was hosing down the
vegetables. He made the lettuce look fresher than it
was. Little drops of water stood on the broccoli heads
among the green beady buds and were just the same
size.

Orlando, I said, Jack was walking the dog last
week at 2 a.m. and I was out at 7 a.m. and you were
here both times.

That's true, he said. I was.

Orlando, how can you do that, how can you get to work, how can you live? How can you see your kids and your wife?

I can't, he said. Maybe once a week.

Are you all right?

Yes. He put down his hose and took my hand in his. You see, he said, this is wonderful work. This is food. I love all work that has to do with food. I'm lucky. He dropped my hand and patted a red cabbage. Look at me, I'm a small businessman. I got an A&P on one side, a Bohack on another, and a fancy International full of cheese and herring down the block. If I don't put in sixteen hours a day I'm dead. But Mrs. A., just look at that rack, the beans, that corner with all the parsley and the arugula and the dill, it's beautiful, right?

Oh yes, I said, I guess it is, but what *I* really love are the little bunches of watercress—the way you've lined the carrot bin with them.

Yeah, Mrs. A., you're O.K. You got the idea. The beauty! he said, and went off to take three inferior strawberries out of a perfect box. A couple of years later—in the present, which I have not quite mentioned (but will)—we fought over Chilean plums. We parted. I was forced to shop in the reasonable supermarket among disinterested people with no credit asked and none offered. But at that particular moment we were at peace. That is, I owed him $275 and he allowed it.

O.K., said Jack, if you and Orlando are such pals,

why aren't all these strawberries ripe? He picked up a rather green eroded one. I invented an anthropological reply. Well, Orlando's father is an old man. One of the jobs Orlando's culture has provided for his father's old age is the sorting of strawberries into pint and quart boxes. Just to be fair, he has to hide one or two greenish ones in each box.

I think I'll go to bed, said Jack.

I was only extrapolating from his article in the third issue of *The Social Ordure*—"Food Merchandising, or Who Invented the Greedy Consumer." I reminded him of this.

He said politely, Ah . . .

The day had been too long and I hadn't said one word about the New Young Fathers or my meeting with Zagrowsky the Pharmacist. I thought we might discuss them at breakfast.

So we slept, his arms around me as sweetly as after the long day he had probably slept beside his former wife (and I as well beside my etc. etc. etc.). I was so comfortable; our good mattress and our nice feelings were such a cozy combination that I remembered a song my friend Ruthy had made up about ten years earlier to tease the time, the place, us:

oh, the marriage bed, the marriage bed
can you think of anything nicer
for days and nights of years and years
you lie beside your darling
your arms are hugging one another

your legs are twined together
until the dark and certain day
your lover comes to take you
   away   away   away

At about 3 a.m. Jack cried out in terror. That's
O.K., kid, I said, you're not the only one. Everybody's mortal. I leaned all my softening strength
against his skinny back. Then I dreamed the following in a kind of diorama of Technicolor abstraction
—that the children had grown all the way up. One
had moved to another neighborhood, the other to a
distant country. *That* one was never to be seen again,
the dream explained, because he had blown up a
very bad bank, and in the dream I was the one
who'd told him to do it. The dream continued; no—
it circled itself, widening into my very old age. Then
his disappearance made one of those typical spiral-
ing descents influenced by film technique. Unreach-
able at the bottom, their childhood played war and
made jokes.

I woke. Where's the glass of water, I screamed. I
want to tell you something, Jack.

What? What? What? He saw my wide-awake
eyes. He sat up. What?

Jack, I want to have a baby.

Ha ha, he said. You can't. Too late. A couple of
years too late, he said, and fell asleep. Then he
spoke. Besides, suppose it worked; I mean, suppose a
miracle. The kid might be very smart, get a scholar-
ship to M.I.T. and get caught up in problem solving

and godalmighty it could invent something worse than anything us old dodos ever imagined. Then he fell asleep and snored.

I pulled the Old Testament out from under the bed where I keep most of my bedtime literature. I jammed an extra pillow under my neck and sat up almost straight in order to read the story of Abraham and Sarah with interlinear intelligence. There was a lot in what Jack said—he often makes a sensible or thought-provoking remark. Because you know how that old story ends—well! With those three monotheistic horsemen of perpetual bossdom and war: Christianity, Judaism, and Islam.

Just the same, I said to softly snoring Jack, before all that popular badness wedged its way into the world, there *was first* the little baby Isaac. You know what I mean: looking at Sarah just like all our own old babies—remember the way they practiced their five little senses. Oh, Jack, that Isaac, Sarah's boy— before he was old enough to be taken out by his father to get his throat cut, he must have just lain around smiling and making up diphthongs and listening, and the women sang songs to him and wrapped him up in such pretty rugs. Right?

In his sleep, which is as contentious as his waking, Jack said yes—but he should not have been allowed to throw all that sand at his brother.

You're right, you're right. I'm with you there, I said. Now all you have to do is be with me.

This Is a Story
about My Friend George,
the Toy Inventor

He is a man of foreign parentage who suffers waves of love, salty tears that crest in his eyes. The shores attacked by those waves are often his children. This isn't a story about his children.

One day, George failed. He had had many successes, so the failure was not a life failure. It was the failure of a half year's work and included, as failure often does, an important loss of income.

He had invented a pinball machine. When we saw it, we said, George! This is not a pinball machine alone. This is the poem of a pinball machine, the essence made delicately concrete, and so forth.

This is what it looked like: Instead of hard metal balls which are propelled into a box with decorated flashing lights and illuminated athletes and planets, balls of blue water are shot into the box. The blue water breaks and scatters in tiny blue droplets of varying volume. The action is swift, the sky-blue droplets skitter and collect again on the magnetic white ground. There are resting places with numbers for scoring.

It is certainly beautiful and stands so far ahead of its time that we were not surprised to learn it had been rejected. After the rejection, George rented a couple of ordinary pinball machines (because he's a serious person, an inventor, an artist) in order to try to understand his failure. He installed them in the boys' attic room. The family played and investigated them for several weeks. Then, to his sorrow, he added understanding and amazement.

How could he have believed he was the one to improve on the pinball machine, that old invention of cumulative complication. He had offered only a small innovation.

Beauty! we said. Bringing all our political theory to bear on the matter, we suggested that there was money to be extracted—even from that—inside the opportunistic life of coopting capitalism.

No, George said, you don't understand. The pinball machine—any pinball machine you play in any penny arcade—is so remarkable, so fine, so shrewdly threaded. It is already beautiful in necessity and sufficiency of wire, connection, possibility.

No, no, George said. The company was right. They gave me six months to make a better pinball machine. They were fair. What gall I had to think I could. No, they were fair. It's as though I had expected to invent the violin.

Zagrowsky Tells

I was standing in the park under that tree. They
call it the Hanging Elm. Once upon a time it made
a big improvement on all kinds of hooligans. Nowadays if, once in a while . . . No. So this woman comes
up to me, a woman minus a smile. I said to my
grandson, Uh oh, Emanuel. Here comes a lady, she
was once a beautiful customer of mine in the pharmacy I showed you.

Emanuel says, Grandpa, who?

She looks O.K. now, but not so hot. Well, what
can you do, time takes a terrible toll off the ladies.

This is her idea of a hello: Iz, what are you doing
with that black child? Then she says, Who is he?
Why are you holding on to him like that? She gives
me a look like God in judgment. You could see it in
famous paintings. Then she says, Why are you yelling at that poor kid?

What yelling? A history lesson about the park.

This is a tree in guide books. How are you by the way, Miss . . . Miss . . . I was embarrassed. I forgot her name absolutely.

Well, who is he? You got him pretty scared.

Me? Don't be ridiculous. It's my grandson. Say hello, Emanuel, don't put on an act.

Emanuel shoves his hand in my pocket to be a little more glued to me. Are you going to open your mouth sonny, yes or no?

She says, Your grandson? Really, Iz, your grandson? What do you mean, your grandson?

Emanuel closes his eyes tight. Did you ever notice children get all mixed up? They don't want to hear about something, they squinch up their eyes. Many children do this.

Now listen Emanuel, I want you to tell this lady who is the smartest boy in kindergarten.

Not a word.

Goddamnit, open your eyes. It's something new with him. Tell her who is the smartest boy—he was just five, he can already read a whole book by himself.

He stands still. He's thinking. I know his little cute mind. Then he jumps up and down yelling, Me me me. He makes a little dance. His grandma calls it his smartness dance. My other ones (three children grown up for some time already) were also very smart, but they don't hold a candle to this character. Soon as I get a chance, I'm gonna bring him to the city to Hunter for gifted children; he should get a test.

But this Miss . . . Miss . . . she's not finished with

us yet. She's worried. Whose kid is he? You adopt him?

Adopt? At my age? It's Cissy's kid. You know my Cissy? I see she knows something. Why not, I had a public business. No surprise.

Of course I remember Cissy. She says this, her face is a little more ironed out.

So, my Cissy, if you remember, she was a nervous girl.

I'll *bet* she was.

Is that a nice way to answer? Cissy *was* nervous . . . The nervousness, to be truthful, ran in Mrs. Z.'s family. Ran? Galloped . . . tarum tarum tarum.

When we were young I used to go over there to visit, and while me and her brother and uncles played pinochle, in the kitchen the three aunts would sit drinking tea. Everything was Oi! Oi! Oi! What for? Nothing to oi about. They got husbands . . . Perfectly fine gentlemen. One in business, two of them real professionals. They just got in the habit somehow. So I said to Mrs. Z., one oi out of you and it's divorce.

I remember your wife very well, this lady says. *Very* well. She puts on the same face like before; her mouth gets small. Your wife *is* a beautiful woman.

So . . . would I marry a mutt?

But she was right. My Nettie when she was young, she was very fair, like some Polish Jews you see once in a while. Like for instance maybe some big blond peasant made a pogrom on her great-grandma.

So I answered her, Oh yes, very nice-looking; even

now she's not so bad, but a little bit on the grouchy side.

O.K., she makes a big sigh like I'm a hopeless case. What did happen to Cissy?

Emanuel, go over there and play with those kids. No? No.

Well, I'll tell you, it's the genes. The genes are the most important. Environment is O.K. But the genes . . . that's where the whole story is written down. I think the school had something to do with it also. She's more an artist like your husband. Am I thinking of the right guy? When she was a kid you should of seen her. She's a nice-looking girl now, even when she has an attack. But then she was something. The family used to go to the mountains in the summer. We went dancing, her and me. What a dancer. People were surprised. Sometimes we danced until 2 a.m.

I don't think that was good, she says. I wouldn't dance with my son all night . . .

Naturally, you're a mother. But "good," who knows what's good? Maybe a doctor. I could have been a doctor, by the way. Her brother-in-law in business would of backed me. But then what? You don't have the time. People call you day and night. I cured more people in a day than a doctor in a week. Many an M.D. called me, said, Zagrowsky, does it work . . . that Parke-Davis medication they put out last month, or it's a fake? I got immediate experience and I'm not too stuck up to tell.

Oh, Iz, you are, she said. She says this like she

means it but it makes her sad. How do I know this? Years in a store. You observe. You watch. The customer is always right, but plenty of times you know he's wrong and also a goddamn fool.

All of a sudden I put her in a certain place. Then I said to myself, Iz, why are you standing here with this woman? I looked her straight in the face and I said, Faith? Right? Listen to me. Now you listen, because I got a question. Is it true, no matter what time you called, even if I was closing up, I came to your house with the penicillin or the tetracycline later? You lived on the fourth-floor walk-up. Your friend what's-her-name, Susan, with the three girls next door? I can see it very clear. Your face is all smeared up with crying, your kid got 105°, maybe more, burning up, you didn't want to leave him in the crib screaming, you're standing in the hall, it's dark. You were living alone, am I right? So young. Also your husband, he comes to my mind, very jumpy fellow, in and out, walking around all night. He drank? I betcha. Irish? Imagine you didn't get along so you got a divorce. Very simple. You kids knew how to live.

She doesn't even answer me. She says . . . you want to know what she says? She says, Oh shit! Then she says, Of course I remember. God, my Richie was sick! Thanks, she says, thanks, god-almighty thanks.

I was already thinking something else: The mind makes its own business. When she first came up to me, I couldn't remember. I knew her well, but where? Then out of no place, a word, her bossy face maybe, exceptionally round, which is not usual, her dark apartment, the four flights, the other girls—all once lively, young . . . you could see them walking around on a sunny day, dragging a couple kids, a carriage, a bike, beautiful girls, but tired from all day, mostly divorced, going home alone? Boyfriends? Who knows how that type lives? I had a big appreciation for them. Sometimes, five o'clock I stood in the door to see them. They were mostly the way models *should* be. I mean not skinny—round, like they were made of little cushions and bigger cushions, depending where you looked; young mothers. I hollered a few words to them, they hollered back. Especially I remember her friend Ruthy —she had two little girls with long black braids, down to here. I told her, In a couple of years, Ruthy, you'll have some beauties on your hands. You better keep an eye on them. In those days the women always answered you in a pleasant way, not afraid to smile. Like this: They said, You really think so? Thanks, Iz.

But this is all used-to-be and in that place there is not only good but bad and the main fact in regard to *this* particular lady: I did her good but to me she didn't always do so much good.

So we stood around a little. Emanuel says, Grandpa, let's go to the swings. Go yourself—it's not so far, there's kids, I see them. No, he says, and stuffs his hand in my pocket again. So don't go— Ach, what a day, I said. Buds and everything. She says,

That's a catalpa tree over there. No kidding! I say.
What do you call that one, doesn't have a single
leaf? Locust, she says. Two locusts, I say.

Then I take a deep breath: O.K.—you still listening? Let me ask you, if I did you so much good
including I saved your baby's life, how come you
did *that*? You know what I'm talking about. A perfectly nice day. I look out the window of the pharmacy and I see four customers, that I seen at least
two in their bathrobes crying to me in the middle of
the night, Help help! They're out there with signs.
ZAGROWSKY IS A RACIST. YEARS AFTER ROSA PARKS,
ZAGROWSKY REFUSES TO SERVE BLACKS. It's like an
etching right *here*. I point out to her my heart. I
know exactly where it is.

She's naturally very uncomfortable when I tell
her. Listen, she says, we were right.

I grab on to Emanuel. You?

Yes, we wrote a letter first, did you answer it? We
said, Zagrowsky, come to your senses. Ruthy wrote
it. We said we would like to talk to you. We tested
you. At least four times, you kept Mrs. Green and
Josie, our friend Josie, who was kind of Spanish
black . . . she lived on the first floor in our house . . .
you kept them waiting a long time till everyone
ahead of them was taken care of. Then you were
very rude, I mean nasty, you can be extremely
nasty, Iz. And then Josie left the store, she called you
some pretty bad names. You remember?

No, I happen not to remember. There was plenty
of yelling in the store. People *really* suffering; come

in yelling for codeine or what to do their mother
was dying. That's what I remember, not some crazy
Spanish lady hollering.

But listen, she says—like all this is not in front of
my eyes, like the past is only a piece of paper in the
yard—you didn't finish with Cissy.

Finish? *You* almost finished my business and
don't think that Cissy didn't hold it up to me. Later
when she was so sick.

Then I thought, Why should I talk to this woman.
I see myself: how I was standing that day how many
years ago?—like an idiot behind the counter waiting
for customers. Everybody is peeking in past the
picket line. It's the kind of neighborhood, if they see
a picket line, half don't come in. The cops say they
have a right. To destroy a person's business. I was
disgusted but I went into the street. After all, I knew
the ladies. I tried to explain, Faith, Ruthy, Mrs.
Kratt—a stranger comes into the store, naturally you
have to serve the old customers first. Anyone would
do the same. Also, they sent in black people, brown
people, all colors, and to tell the truth I didn't like
the idea my pharmacy should get the reputation of
being a cut-rate place for them. They move into a
neighborhood . . . I did what everyone did. Not to
insult people too much, but to discourage them a
little, they shouldn't feel so welcome. They could
just move in because it's a nice area.

All right. A person looks at my Emanuel and says,
Hey! he's not altogether from the white race, what's
going on? I'll tell you what: life is going on. You

have an opinion. I have an opinion. Life don't have
no opinion.

I moved away from this Faith lady. I didn't like
to be near her. I sat down on the bench. I'm no
spring chicken. Cock-a-doodle-do, I only holler once
in a while. I'm tired, I'm mostly the one in charge
of our Emanuel. Mrs. Z. stays home, her legs swell
up. It's a shame.

In the subway once she couldn't get off at the
right stop. The door opens, she can't get up. She tried
(she's a little overweight). She says to a big guy
with a notebook, a big colored fellow, Please help
me get up. He says to her, You kept me down three
hundred years, you can stay down another ten minutes. I asked her, Nettie, didn't you tell him we're
raising a little boy brown like a coffee bean. But he's
right, says Nettie, we done that. We kept them
down.

We? We? My two sisters and my father were
being fried up for Hitler's supper in 1944 and you
say we?

Nettie sits down. Please bring me some tea. Yes,
Iz, I say: *We.*

I can't even put up the water I'm so mad. You
know, my Mrs., you are crazy like your three aunts,
crazy like our Cissy. Your whole family put in the
genes to make it for sure that she wouldn't have a
chance. Nettie looks at me. She says, Ai ai. She
doesn't say oi anymore. She got herself assimilated
into ai . . . That's how come she also says "we" done
it. Don't think this will make you an American, I

said to her, that you included yourself in with
Robert E. Lee. Naturally it was a joke, only what is
there to laugh?

I'm tired right now. This Faith could even see I'm
a little shaky. What should she do, she's thinking.
But she decides the discussion ain't over so she sits
down sideways. The bench is damp. It's only April.

What about Cissy? Is she all right?

It ain't your business how she is.

O.K. She starts to go.

Wait wait! Since I seen you in your nightgown a
couple of times when you were a handsome young
woman . . . She really gets up this time. I think she
must be a woman's libber, they don't like remarks
about nightgowns. Bathrobes, she didn't mind. Let
her go! The hell with her . . . but she comes back.
She says, Once and for all, cut it out, Iz. I really
want to know. Is Cissy all right?

You want. She's fine. She lives with me and
Nettie. She's in charge of the plants. It's an all-day
job.

But why should I leave her off the hook. Oh boy,
Faith, I got to say it, what you people put on me!
And you want to know how Cissy is. *You!* Why?
Sure. You remember you finished with the picket
lines after a week or two. I don't know why. Tired?
Summer maybe, you got to go away, make trouble
at the beach. But I'm stuck there. Did I have air con-
ditioning yet? All of a sudden I see Cissy outside.
She has a sign also. She must've got the idea from
you women. A big sandwich board, she walks up

and down. If someone talks to her, she presses her mouth together.

I don't remember that, Faith says.

Of course, you were already on Long Island or Cape Cod or someplace—the Jersey shore.

No, she says, I was not. I was not. (I see this is a big insult to her that she should go away for the summer.)

Then I thought, Calm down, Zagrowsky. Because for a fact I didn't want her to leave, because, since I already began to tell, I have to tell the whole story. I'm not a person who keeps things in. Tell! That opens up the congestion a little—the lungs are for breathing, not secrets. My wife never tells, she coughs, coughs. All night. Wakes up. Ai, Iz, open up the window, there's no air. You poor woman, if you want to breathe, you got to tell.

So I said to this Faith, I'll tell you how Cissy is but you got to hear the whole story how we suffered. I thought, O.K. Who cares! Let her get on the phone later with the other girls. They should know what they started.

How we took our own Cissy from here to there to the biggest doctor—I had good contacts from the pharmacy. Dr. Francis O'Connel, the heavy Irishman over at the hospital, sat with me and Mrs. Z. for two hours, a busy man. He explained that it was one of the most great mysteries. They were ignoramuses, the most brilliant doctors were dummies in this field. But still, in my place, I heard of this cure and that one. So we got her massaged fifty times

from head to toe, whatever someone suggested. We
stuffed her with vitamins and minerals—there was a
real doctor in charge of this idea.

If she would take the vitamins—sometimes she
shut her mouth. To her mother she said dirty words.
We weren't used to it. Meanwhile, in front of my
place every morning, she walks up and down. She
could of got minimum wage, she was so regular.
Her afternoon job is to follow my wife from corner
to corner to tell what my wife done wrong to her
when she was a kid. Then after a couple months, all
of a sudden she starts to sing. She has a beautiful
voice. She took lessons from a well-known person.
On Christmas week, in front of the pharmacy she
sings half the *Messiah* by Handel. You know it? So
that's nice, you think. Oh, that's beautiful. But
where were you you didn't notice that she don't
have on a coat. You didn't see she walks up and
down, her socks are falling off? Her face and hands
are like she's the super in the cellar. She sings! she
sings! Two songs she sings the most: one is about the
Gentiles will see the light and the other is, Look! a
virgin will conceive a son. My wife says, Sure,
naturally, she wishes she was a married woman just
like anyone. Baloney. She could of. She had plenty
of dates. Plenty. She sings, the idiots applaud, some
skunk yells, Go, Cissy, go. What? Go where? Some
days she just hollers.

Hollers what?

Oh, I forgot about you. Hollers anything. Hollers,
Racist! Hollers, He sells poison chemicals! Hollers,

He's a terrible dancer, he got three left legs! (Which isn't true, just to insult me publicly, plain silly.) The people laugh. What'd she say? Some didn't hear so well; hollers, You go to whores. Also not true. She met me once with a woman actually a distant relative from Israel. Everything is in her head. It's a garbage pail.

One day her mother says to her, Cissile, comb your hair, for godsakes, darling. For this remark, she gives her mother a sock in the face. I come home I see a woman not at all young with two black eyes and a bloody nose. The doctor said, Before it's better with your girl, it's got to be worse. That much he knew. He sent us to a beautiful place, a hospital right at the city line—I'm not sure if it's Westchester or the Bronx, but thank God, you could use the subway. That's how I found out what I was saving up my money for. I thought for retiring in Florida to walk around under the palm trees in the middle of the week. Wrong. It was for my beautiful Cissy, she should have a nice home with other crazy people.

So little by little, she calms down. We can visit her. She shows us the candy store, we give her a couple of dollars; soon our life is this way. Three times a week my wife goes, gets on the subway with delicious foods (no sugar, they're against sugar); she brings something nice, a blouse or a kerchief—a present, you understand, to show love; and once a week I go, but she don't want to look at me. So close we were, like sweethearts—you can imagine how I feel. Well, you have children so you know, little

children little troubles, big children big troubles—
it's a saying in Yiddish. Maybe the Chinese said it
too.

Oh, Iz. How could it happen like that? All of a
sudden. No signs?

What's with this Faith? Her eyes are full of tears.
Sensitive I suppose. I see what she's thinking. Her
kids are teenagers. So far they look O.K. but what
will happen? People think of themselves. Human
nature. At least she doesn't tell me it's my wife's
fault or mine. I did something terrible! I loved my
child. I know what's on people's minds. I know
psychology *very* well. Since this happened to us, I
read up on the whole business.

Oh, Iz . . .

She puts her hand on my knee. I look at her.
Maybe she's just a nut. Maybe she thinks I'm plain
old (I almost am). Well, I said it before. Thank God
for the head. Inside the head is the only place you
got to be young when the usual place gets used up.
For some reason she gives me a kiss on the cheek. A
peculiar person.

Faith, I still can't figure it out why you girls were
so rotten to me.

But we were right.

Then this lady Queen of Right makes a small
lecture. She don't remember my Cissy walking up
and down screaming bad language but she remem-
bers: After Mrs. Kendrick's big fat snotty maid
walked out with Kendrick's allergy order, I made a
face and said, Ho ho! the great lady! That's terrible?

She says whenever I saw a couple walk past on the block, a black-and-white couple, I said, Ugh—disgusting! It shouldn't be allowed! She heard this remark from me a few times. So? It's a matter of taste. Then she tells me about this Josie, probably Puerto Rican, once more—the one I didn't serve in time. Then she says, Yeah, and really, Iz, what about Emanuel?

Don't you look at Emanuel, I said. Don't you dare. He has nothing to do with it.

She rolls her eyes around and around a couple of times. She got more to say. She also doesn't like how I talk to women. She says I called Mrs. Z. a grizzly bear a few times. It's my wife, no? That I was winking and blinking at the girls, a few pinches. A lie . . . maybe I patted, but I never pinched. Besides, I know for a fact a couple of them loved it. She says, No. None of them liked it. Not one. They only put up with it because it wasn't time yet in history to holler. (An American-born girl has some nerve to mention history.)

But, she says, Iz, forget all that. I'm sorry you have so much trouble now. She really is sorry. But in a second she changes her mind. She's not so sorry. She takes her hand back. Her mouth makes a little O.

Emanuel climbs up on my lap. He pats my face. Don't be sad, Grandpa, he says. He can't stand if he sees a tear on a person's face. Even a stranger. If his mama gets a black look, he's smart, he doesn't go to her anymore. He comes to my wife. Grandma, he says, my poor mama is very sad. My wife jumps up and runs in. Worried. Scared. Did Cissy take her pills? What's going on? Once, he went to Cissy and said, Mama, why are you crying? So this is her answer to a little boy: she stands up straight and starts to bang her head on the wall. Hard.

My mama! he screams. Lucky I was home. Since then he goes straight to his grandma for his troubles. What will happen? We're not so young. My oldest son is doing extremely well—only he lives in a very exclusive neighborhood in Rockland County. Our other boy—well, he's in his own life, he's from that generation. He went away.

She looks at me, this Faith. She can't say a word. She sits there. She opens her mouth almost. I know what she wants to know. How did Emanuel come into the story. When?

Then she says to me exactly those words. Well, where does Emanuel fit in?

He fits, he fits. Like a golden present from Nasser. Nasser?

O.K., Egypt, not Nasser—he's from Isaac's other son, get it? A close relation. I was sitting one day thinking, Why? why? The answer: To remind us. That's the purpose of most things.

It was Abraham, she interrupts me. He had two sons, Isaac and Ishmael. God promised him he would be the father of generations; he was. But you know, she says, he wasn't such a good father to those two little boys. Not so unusual, she has to add on.

You see! That's what they make of the Bible,

those women; because they got it in for men. Of
course I meant Abraham. Abraham. Did I say Isaac?
Once in a while I got to admit it, she says something
true. You remember one son he sent out of the house
altogether, the other he was ready to chop up if he
only heard a noise in his head saying, Go! Chop!

But the question is, Where did Emanuel fit. I
didn't mind telling. I wanted to tell, I explained that
already.

So it begins. One day my wife goes to the admin-
istration of Cissy's hospital and she says, What kind
of a place you're running here. I have just looked at
my daughter. A blind person could almost see it.
My daughter is pregnant. What goes on here at
night? Who's the supervisor? Where is she this
minute?

Pregnant? they say like they never heard of it.
And they run around and the regular doctor comes
and says, Yes, pregnant. Sure. You got more news?
my wife says. And then: meetings with the weekly
psychiatrist, the day-by-day psychologist, the nerve
doctor, the social worker, the supervising nurse, the
nurse's aide. My wife says, Cissy knows. She's not
an idiot, only mixed up and depressed. She *knows*
she has a child in her womb inside of her like a
normal woman. She likes it, my wife said. She even
said to her, Mama, I'm having a baby, and she gave
my wife a kiss. The first kiss in a couple of years.
How do you like that?

Meanwhile, they investigated thoroughly. It

turns out the man is a colored fellow. One of the gardeners. But he left a couple months ago for the Coast. I could imagine what happened. Cissy always loved flowers. When she was a little girl she was planting seeds every minute and sitting all day in front of the flower pot to see the little flower cracking up the seed. So she must of watched him and watched him. He dug up the earth. He put in the seeds. She watches.

The office apologized. Apologized? An accident. The supervisor was on vacation that week. I could sue them for a million dollars. Don't think I didn't talk to a lawyer. That time, then, when I heard, I called a detective agency to find him. My plan was to kill him. I would tear him limb from limb. What to do next. They called them all in again. The psychiatrist, the psychologist, they only left out the nurse's aide.

The only hope she could live a half-normal life— not in the institutions: she must have this baby, she could carry it full term. No, I said, I can't stand it. I refuse. Out of my Cissy, who looked like a piece of gold, would come a black child. Then the psychologist says, Don't be so bigoted. What nerve! Little by little my wife figured out a good idea. O.K., well, we'll put it out for adoption. Cissy doesn't even have to see it in person.

You are laboring under a misapprehension, says the boss of the place. They talk like that. What he meant, he meant we got to take that child home with us and if we really loved Cissy . . . Then he

gave us a big lecture on this baby: it's Cissy's connection to life; also, it happens she was crazy about
this gardener, this son of a bitch, a black man with
a green thumb.

You see I can crack a little joke because look at
this pleasure. I got a little best friend here. Where I
go, he goes, even when I go down to the Italian side
of the park to play a little bocce with the old goats
over there. They invite me if they see me in the
supermarket: Hey, Iz! Tony's sick. You come on an'
play, O.K.? My wife says, Take Emanuel, he should
see how men play games. I take him, those old guys
they also seen plenty in their day. They think I'm
some kind of a do-gooder. Also, a lot of those people
are ignorant. They think the Jews are a little bit
colored anyways, so they don't look at him too long.
He goes to the swings and they make believe they
never even seen him.

I didn't mean to get off the subject. What is the
subject? The subject is how we took the baby. My
wife, Mrs. Z., Nettie, she plain forced me. She said,
We got to take this child on us. I will move out of
here into the project with Cissy and be on welfare.
Iz, you better make up your mind. Her brother, a
top social worker, he encouraged her, I think he's a
Communist also, the way he talks the last twenty,
thirty years . . .

He says: You'll live, Iz. It's a baby, after all. It's
got your blood in it. Unless of course you want Cissy
to rot away in that place till you're so poor they
don't keep her anymore. Then they'll stuff her into

Bellevue or Central Islip or something. First she's a zombie, then she's a vegetable. That's what you want, Iz?

After this conversation I get sick. I can't go to work. Meanwhile, every night Nettie cries. She don't get dressed in the morning. She walks around with a broom. Doesn't sweep up. Starts to sweep, bursts into tears. Puts a pot of soup on the stove, runs into the bedroom, lies down. Soon I think I'll have to put her away too.

I give in.

My listener says to me, Right, Iz, you did the right thing. What else could you do?

I feel like smacking her. I'm not a violent person, just very excitable, but who asked her?—Right, Iz. She sits there looking at me, nodding her head from rightness. Emanuel is finally in the playground. I see him swinging and swinging. He could swing for two hours. He likes that. He's a regular swinger.

Well, the bad part of the story is over. Now is the good part. Naming the baby. What should we name him? Little brown baby. An intermediate color. A perfect stranger.

In the maternity ward, you know where the mothers lie, with the new babies, Nettie is saying, Cissy, Cissile darling, my sweetest heart (this is how my wife talked to her, like she was made of gold—or eggshells), my darling girl, what should we name this little child?

Cissy is nursing. On her white flesh is this little black curly head. Cissy says right away: Emanuel.

Immediately. When I hear this, I say, Ridiculous. Ridiculous, such a long Jewish name on a little baby. I got old uncles with such names. Then they all get called Manny. Uncle Manny. Again she says— Emanuel!

David is nice, I suggest in a kind voice. It's your grandpa's, he should rest in peace. Michael is nice too, my wife says. Joshua is beautiful. Many children have these beautiful names nowadays. They're nice modern names. People like to say them.

No, she says, Emanuel. Then she starts screaming, Emanuel Emanuel. We almost had to give her extra pills. But we were careful on account of the milk. The milk could get affected.

O.K., everyone hollered. O.K. Calm yourself, Cissy. O.K. Emanuel. Bring the birth certificate. Write it down. Put it down. Let her see it. Emanuel . . . In a few days, the rabbi came. He raised up his eyebrows a couple times. Then he did his job, which is to make the bris. In other words, a circumcision. This is done so the child will be a man in Israel. That's the expression they use. He isn't the first colored child. They tell me long ago we were mostly dark. Also, now I think of it, I wouldn't mind going over there to Israel. They say there are plenty black Jews. It's not unusual over there at all. They ought to put out more publicity on it. Because I have to think where he should live. Maybe it won't be so good for him here. Because my son, his fancy ideas . . . ach, forget it.

What about the building, your neighborhood, I

mean where you live now? Are there other black
people in the community?

Oh yeah, but they're very snobbish. Don't ask
what they got to be so snobbish.

Because, she says, he should have friends his own
color, he shouldn't have the burden of being the only
one in school.

Listen, it's New York, it's not Oshkosh, Wisconsin.
But she gets going, you can't stop her.

After all, she says, he should eventually know his
own people. It's their life he'll have to share. I know
it's a problem to you, Iz, I know, but that's the way
it is. A friend of mine with the same situation moved
to a more integrated neighborhood.

Is that a fact? I say, Where's that?

Oh, there are . . .

I start to tell her, Wait a minute, we live thirty-
five years in this apartment. But I can't talk. I sit
very quietly for a while, I think and think. I say to
myself, Be like a Hindu, Iz, calm like a cucumber.
But it's too much. Listen, Miss, Miss Faith—do me a
favor, don't teach me.

I'm not teaching you, Iz, it's just . . .

Don't answer me every time I say something.
Talking talking. It's true. What for? To whom?
Why? Nettie's right. It's our business. She's telling
me Emanuel's life.

You don't know nothing about it, I yell at her. Go
make a picket line. Don't teach me.

She gets up and looks at me kind of scared. Take
it easy, Iz.

Zagrowsky Tells

Emanuel is coming. He hears me. He got his little worried face. She sticks out a hand to pat him, his grandpa is hollering so loud.

But I can't put up with it. Hands off, I yell. It ain't your kid. Don't lay a hand on him. And I grab his shoulder and push him through the park, past the playground and the big famous arch. She runs after me a minute. Then she sees a couple friends. Now she has what to talk about. Three, four women. They make a little bunch. They talk. They turn around, they look. One waves. Hiya, Iz.

This park is full of noise. Everybody got something to say to the next guy. Playing this music, standing on their heads, juggling—someone even brought a piano, can you believe it, some job.

I sold the store four years ago. I couldn't put in the work no more. But I wanted to show Emanuel my pharmacy, what a beautiful place it was, how it sent three children to college, saved a couple lives— imagine: one store!

I tried to be quiet for the boy. You want ice cream, Emanuel? Here's a dollar, sonny. Buy yourself a Good Humor. The man's over there. Don't forget to ask for the change. I bend down to give him a kiss. I don't like that he heard me yell at a woman and my hand is still shaking. He runs a few steps, he looks back to make sure I didn't move an inch.

I got my eye on him too. He waves a chocolate popsicle. It's a little darker than him. Out of that crazy mob a young fellow comes up to me. He has a baby strapped on his back. That's the style now. He asks like it's an ordinary friendly question, points to Emanuel. Gosh what a cute kid. Whose is he? I don't answer. He says it again, Really some cute kid.

I just look in his face. What does he want? I should tell him the story of my life? I don't need to tell. I already told and told. So I said very loud—no one else should bother me—how come it's your business, mister? Who do you think he is? By the way, whose kid you got on your back? It don't look like you.

He says, Hey there buddy, be cool be cool. I didn't mean anything. (You met anyone lately who meant something when he opened his mouth?) While I'm hollering at him, he starts to back away. The women are gabbing in a little clutch by the statue. It's a considerable distance, lucky they got radar. They turn around sharp like birds and fly over to the man. They talk very soft. Why are you bothering this old man, he got enough trouble? Why don't you leave him alone?

The fellow says, I wasn't bothering him. I just asked him something.

Well, he thinks you're bothering him, Faith says.

Then her friend, a woman maybe forty, very angry, starts to holler, How come you don't take care of your own kid? She's crying. Are you deaf? Naturally the third woman makes a remark, doesn't want to be left out. She taps him on his jacket: I seen you around here before, buster, you better watch out. He walks away from them backwards. They start in shaking hands.

Then this Faith comes back to me with a big smile. She says, Honestly, some people are a pain, aren't they, Iz? We sure let him have it, didn't we? And she gives me one of her kisses. Say hello to Cissy—O.K.? She puts her arms around her pals. They say a few words back and forth, like cranking up a motor. Then they bust out laughing. They wave goodbye to Emanuel. Laughing. Laughing. So long, Iz . . . see you . . .

So I say, What is going on, Emanuel, could you explain to me what just happened? Did you notice anywhere a joke? This is the first time he doesn't answer me. He's writing his name on the sidewalk. EMANUEL. Emanuel in big capital letters.

And the women walk away from us. Talking. Talking.

The Expensive Moment

Faith did not tell Jack.

At about two in the afternoon she went to visit Nick Hegstraw, the famous sinologist. He was not famous in the whole world. He was famous in their neighborhood and in the adjoining neighborhoods, north, south, and east. He was studying China, he said, in order to free us all of distance and mystery. But because of foolish remarks that were immediately published, he had been excluded from wonderful visits to China's new green parlor. He sometimes felt insufficiently informed. Hundreds of people who knew nothing about Han and Da tung visited, returned, wrote articles; one friend with about seventy-five Chinese words had made a three-hour documentary. Well, sometimes he did believe in socialism and sometimes only in the Late T'ang. It's hard to stand behind a people and culture in revolutionary transition when you are constantly worried about their irreplaceable and breakable artifacts.

He was noticeably handsome, the way men are every now and then, with a face full of good architectural planning. (Good use of face space, Jack said.) In the hardware store or in line at the local movie, women and men would look at him. They might turn away saying, Not my type, or, Where have I seen him before? TV? Actually they had seen him at the vegetable market. As an unmarried vegetarian sinologist he bought bagfuls of broccoli and waited with other eaters for snow peas from California at $4.79 a pound.

Are you lovers? Ruth asked.

Oh God, no. I'm pretty monogamous when I'm monogamous. Why are you laughing?

You're lying. Really, Faith, why did you describe him at such length? You don't usually do that.

But the fun of talking, Ruthy. What about that? It's as good as fucking lots of times. Isn't it?

Oh boy, Ruth said, if it's that good, then it's got to be that bad.

At lunch Jack said, Ruth is not a Chinese cook. She doesn't mince words. She doesn't sauté a lot of imperial verbs and docile predicates like some women.

Faith left the room. Someday, she said, I'm never coming back.

But I love the way Jack talks, said Ruth. He's a

true gossip like us. And another thing, he's the only one who ever asks me anymore about Rachel.

Don't trust him, said Faith.

After Faith slammed the door, Jack decided to buy a pipe so he could smoke thoughtfully in the evening. He wished he had a new dog or a new child or a new wife. He had none of these things because he only thought about them once in ten days and then only for about five minutes. The interest in sustained shopping or courtship had left him. He was a busy man selling discount furniture in a rough neighborhood during the day, and reading reading reading, thinking writing grieving all night the bad world-ending politics which were using up the last years of his life. Oh, come back, come back, he cried. Faith! At least for supper.

On this particular afternoon, Nick (the sinologist) said, How are your children? Fine, she said. Tonto is in love and Richard has officially joined the League for Revolutionary Youth.

Ah, said Nick. L.R.Y. I spoke at one of their meetings last month. They threw half a pizza pie at me.

Why? What'd you say? Did you say something terrible? Maybe it's an anti-agist coalition of New Left pie throwers and Old Left tomato throwers.

It's not a joke, he said. And it's not funny. And besides, that's not what I want to talk about. He then expressed opposition to the Great Leap Forward and the Cultural Revolution. He did this by walking back and forth muttering, Wrong. Wrong. Wrong.

Faith, who had just read *Fanshen* at his sugges-
tion, accepted both. But he worried about great art
and literature, its way of rising out of the already
risen. Faith, sit down, he said. Where were the already risen nowadays? Driven away from their
typewriters and calligraphy pens by the Young
Guards—like all the young, wild with a dream of
wildness.

Faith said, Maybe it's the right now rising. Maybe
the already risen don't need anything more. They
just sit there in their lawn chairs and appreciate the
culture of the just rising. They may even like to do
that. The work of creation is probably too hard
when you are required because of having already
risen to be always distinguishing good from bad,
great from good . . .

Nick would not even laugh at serious jokes. He
decided to show Faith with mocking examples how
wrong she was. None of the examples convinced her.
In fact, they seemed to support an opposing position. Faith wondered if his acquisitive mind was not
sometimes betrayed by a poor filing system.

Here they are anyway:

Working hard in the fields of Shanxi is John
Keats, brilliant and tubercular. The sun beats on his
pale flesh. The water in which he is ankle-deep is
colder than he likes. The little green shoots are no
comfort to him despite their light-green beauty. He
is thinking about last night—this lunar beauty, etc.
When he gets back to the commune he learns that
they have been requested by the province to write

poems. Keats is discouraged. He's thinking, This
lunar beauty, this lunar beauty . . . The head com-
munard, a bourgeois leftover, says, Oh, what can ail
thee, pale individualist? He laughs, then says, Relax,
comrade. Just let politics take command. Keats does
this, and soon, smiling his sad intelligent smile, he
says, Ah . . .

This lunar beauty
> *touches Shanxi province*
in the year of the bumper crops
> *the peasants free of the landlords*
stand in the fields
> *they talk of this and that*
> *and admire*
the harvest moon.

Meanwhile, all around him peasants are dampen-
ing the dry lead pencil points with their tongues.

Faith interrupted. She hoped someone would tell
them how dangerous lead was. And industrial
pollution.

For godsakes, said Nick, and continued. One
peasant writes:

This morning the paddy
> *looked like the sea*
At high tide we will
> *harvest the rice*
This is because of Mao Zedong
> *whose love for the peasants*
has fed the urban proletariat.

That's enough. Do you get it? Yes, Faith said.
Something like this? And sang.

On the highway to Communism
the little children put plum blossoms
in their hair and dance
on the new-harvested wheat

She was about to remember another poem from
her newly invented memory, but Nick said, Faith,
it's already 3:30, so—full of the play of poems they
unfolded his narrow daybed to a comfortable three-
quarter width. Their lovemaking was ordinary but
satisfactory. Its difference lay only in difference. Of
course, if one is living a whole life in passionate affection with another, this differentness on occasional
afternoons is often enough.

And besides that, almost at once on rising to tea
or coffee, Faith asked, Nick, why do they have such
a rotten foreign policy? The question had settled in
her mind earlier, resting just under the light in-
flammation of desire.

It was not the first time she had asked this question, nor was Nick the last person who answered.

Nick: For godsakes, don't you understand anything about politics?

Richard: Yeah, and why does Israel trade probably every day with South Africa?

Ruth (*Although her remarks actually came a*

couple of years later): Cuba carries on commercial negotiations with Argentina. No?

The boys at supper: Tonto (*Softly, with narrowed eyes*): Why did China recognize Pinochet just about ten minutes after the coup in Chile?

Richard (*Tolerantly explaining*): Asshole, because Allende didn't know how to run a revolution, that's why.

Jack reminded them that the U.S.S.R. may have had to overcome intense ideological repugnance in order to satisfy her old longing for South African industrial diamonds.

Faith thought, But if you think like that forever you can be sad forever. You can be cynical, you can go around saying no hope, you can say import-export, you can mumble all day, World Bank. So she tried thinking: The beauty of trade, the caravans crossing Africa and Asia, the roads to Peru through the terrible forests of Guatemala, and then especially the village markets of underdeveloped countries, plazas behind churches under awnings and tents, not to mention the Orlando Market around the corner; also the Free Market, which costs so much in the world, and what about the discount house of Jack, Son of Jake.

Oh sure, Richard said, the beauty of trade. I'm surprised at you, Ma, the beauty of trade—those Indians going through Guatemala with leather thongs cutting into their foreheads holding about a ton of beauty on their backs. Beauty, he said.

He rested for about an hour. Then he continued. I'm surprised at you Faith, really surprised. He blinked his eyes a couple of times. Mother, he said, have you ever read any political theory? No. All those dumb peace meetings you go to. Don't they ever talk about anything but melting up a couple of really great swords?

He'd become so pale.

Richard, she said. You're absolutely white. You seem to have quit drinking orange juice.

This simple remark made him leave home for three days.

But first he looked at her with either contempt or despair.

Then, because the brain at work pays no attention to time and speedily connects and chooses, she thought: Oh, long ago I looked at my father. What kind of face is that? he had asked. She was leaning against their bedroom wall. She was about fourteen. Fifteen? A lot you care, she said. A giant war is coming out of Germany and all you say is Russia. Bad old Russia. I'm the one that's gonna get killed. You? he answered. Ha ha! A little girl sitting in safe America is going to be killed. Ha ha!

And what about the looks those other boys half a generation ago had made her accept. Ruth had called them put-up-or-shut-up looks. She and her friends had walked round and round the draft boards with signs that said I COUNSEL DRAFT REFUSAL. Some of those young fellows were calm and holy, and some were fierce and grouchy. But not one of them was trivial, and neither was Richard.

Still, Faith thought, what if history should seize him as it had actually taken Ruth's daughter Rachel when her face was still as round as an apple; a moment in history, the expensive moment when everyone his age is called but just a few are chosen by conscience or passion or even only love of one's own agemates, and they are the ones who smash an important nosecone (as has been recently done) or blow up some building full of oppressive money or murderous military plans; but, oh, what if a human creature (maybe rotten to the core but a living person still) is in it? What if they disappear then to live in exile or in the deepest underground and you don't see them for ten years or have to travel to Cuba or Canada or farther to look at their changed faces? Then you think sadly, I could have worked harder at raising that child, the one that was once mine. I could have raised him to become a brilliant economist or finish graduate school and be a lawyer or a doctor maybe. He could have done a lot of good, just as much *that* way, healing or defending the underdog.

But Richard had slipped a note under the door before he left. In his neat handwriting it said: "Trade. Shit. It's production that's beautiful. That's what's beautiful. And the producers. They're beautiful."

What's the use, said Ruth when she and Faith sat eating barley soup in the Art Foods Deli. You're always wrong. She looked into the light beyond the plate-glass window. It was unusual for her to allow sadness. Faith took her hand and kissed it. She said,

Ruthy darling. Ruth leaned across the table to hug her. The soup spoon fell to the floor, mixing barley and sawdust.

But look, Ruth said, Joe got this news clipping at the office from some place in Minnesota. "Red and green acrylic circles were painted around telephone poles and trees ringing the Dakota State Prison last night. It was assumed that the Red and the Green were planning some destructive act. These circles were last seen in Arizona. Two convicts escaped from that prison within a week. Red and green circles were stenciled on the walls of their cells. The cost for removing these signatures will probably go as high as $4,300."

What for? said Faith.

For? asked Ruth. They were political prisoners. Someone has to not forget them. The green is for ecology.

Nobody leaves that out nowadays.

Well, they shouldn't, said Ruth.

This Rachel of Ruth and Joe's had grown from girl to woman in far absence, making little personal waves from time to time in the newspapers or in rumor which would finally reach her parents on the shores of their always waiting—that is, the office mailbox or the eleven o'clock news.

One day Ruth and Joe were invited to a cultural event. This was because Joe was a cultural worker. He had in fact edited *The Social Ordure*, a periodical which published everything Jack wrote. He and Ruth had also visited China and connected them-

selves in print to some indulgent views of the Gang
of Four, from which it had been hard to disengage.
Ruth was still certain that the bad politics and free
life of Jiang Qing would be used for at least a generation to punish ALL Chinese women.

But isn't that true everywhere, said Faith. If you
say a simple thing like, "There are only eight women
in Congress," or if you say the word "patriarchy,"
someone always says, Yeah? look at Margaret
Thatcher, or look at Golda Meir.

I love Golda Meir.

You do? Oh! said Faith.

But the evening belonged to the Chinese artists
and writers who had been rehabilitated while still
alive. All sorts of American cultural workers were
invited. Some laughed to hear themselves described
in this way. They were accustomed to being called
"dreamer poet realist postmodernist." They might
have liked being called "cultural dreamer," but no
one had thought of that yet.

Many of these Chinese artists (mostly men and
some women) flew back and forth from American
coast to coast so often (sometimes stopping in Iowa
City) that they were no longer interested in window
seats but slept on the aisle or across the fat center
where the armrests can be adjusted . . . while the
great deep dipping Rockies, the Indian Black Hills,
the Badlands, the good and endless plains moved
slowly west under the gently trembling jet. They
never bother anymore to dash to the windows at the
circling of New York as the pattern holds and the
lights of our city engage and eliminate the sky.

Ruth said she would personally bring Nick to the party since China was still too annoyed to have invited him. It wasn't fair for a superficial visitor like herself to be present when a person like Nick, with whole verses of his obsession falling out of his pockets, was excluded.

That's O.K., Ruth. You don't have to ask him, Faith said. Don't bother on my account. I don't even see him much anymore.

How come?

I don't know. Whenever I got to like one of his opinions he'd change it, and he never liked any of mine. Also, I couldn't talk to you about it, so it never got thick enough. I mean woofed and warped. Anyway, it hadn't been Nick, she realized. He was all right, but it was travel she longed for—somewhere else—the sexiness of the unknown parts of far imaginable places.

Sex? Ruth said. She bit her lips. Wouldn't it be interesting if way out there Rachel was having a baby?

God, yes, of course! Wonderful! Oh, Ruthy, Faith said, remembering babies, those round, staring, day-in day-out companions of her youth.

Well, Faith asked, what was he like, Nick—the poet Ai Qing? What'd he say?

He has a very large head, Nick said. The great poet raised from exile.

Was Ding Ling there? The amazing woman, the storyteller, Ding Ling?

They're not up to her yet, Nick said. Maybe next year.

Well, what did Bien Tselin say? Faith asked.
Nick, tell me.

Well, he's very tiny. He looks like my father did
when he was old.

Yes, but what did they say?

Do you have any other questions? he asked. I'm
thinking about something right now. He was writing in his little book—thoughts, comments, maybe
even new songs for Chinese modernization—which
he planned to publish as soon as possible. He thought
Faith could read them then.

Finally he said, They showed me their muscles.
There were other poets there. They told some jokes
but not against us. They laughed and nudged each
other. They talked Chinese, you know. I don't know
why they were so jolly. They kept saying, Do not
think that we have ceased to be Communists. We are
Communists. They weren't bitter. They acted interested and happy.

Ruthy, Faith said, please tell me what they said.

Well, one of the women, Faith, about our age, she
said the same thing. She also said the peasants were
good to her. But the soldiers were bad. She said the
peasants in the countryside helped her. They knew
she felt lonely and frightened. She said she loved the
Chinese peasant. That's exactly the way she said it,
like a little speech: I'll never forget and I will always love the Chinese peasant. It's the one thing
Mao was right about—of course he was also a good
poet. But she said, well, you can imagine—she said,
the children . . . When the entire working office was
sent down to the countryside to dig up stones, she

left her daughters with her mother. Her mother was old-fashioned, especially about girls. It's not so hard to be strong about oneself.

Some months later, at a meeting of women's governmental organizations sponsored by the UN, Faith met the very same Chinese woman who'd talked to Ruth. She remembered Ruth well. Yes, the lady who hasn't seen her daughter in eight years. Oh, what a sadness. Who would forget that woman. I have known a few. My name is Xie Feng, she said. Now you say it.

The two women said each other's strange name and laughed. The Chinese woman said, Faith in what? Then she gathered whatever strength and aggression she'd needed to reach this country; she added the courtesy of shyness, breathed deep, and said, Now I would like to see how you live. I have been to meetings, one after another and day after day. But what is a person's home like? How do you live?

Faith said, Me? My house? You want to see my house? In the mirror that evening brushing her teeth, she smiled at her smiling face. She had been invited to be hospitable to a woman from half the world away who'd lived a life beyond foreignness and had experienced extreme history.

The next day they drank tea in Faith's kitchen out of Chinese cups that Ruth had brought from her travels. Misty terraced hills were painted on these cups and a little oil derrick inserted among them.

The Expensive Moment

Faith showed her the boys' bedroom. The Chinese woman took a little camera out of her pocket. You don't mind? she asked. This is the front room, said Faith. It's called the living room. This is our bedroom. That's a picture of Jack giving a paper at the Other Historian meeting and that picture is Jack with two guys who've worked in his store since they were all young. The skinny one just led a strike against Jack and won. Jack says they were right.

I see—both principled men, said the Chinese woman.

They walked around the block a couple of times to get the feel of a neighborhood. They stopped for strudel at the Art Foods. It was half past two and just in time to see the children fly out of the school around the corner. The littlest ones banged against the legs of teachers and mothers. Here and there a father rested his length against somebody's illegally parked car. They stopped to buy a couple of apples. This is my Chinese friend from China, Faith said to Eddie the butcher, who was smoking a cigar, spitting and smiling at the sunlight of an afternoon break. So many peaches, so many oranges, the woman said admiringly to Eddie.

They walked west to the Hudson River. It's called the North River but it's really our Lordly Hudson. This is a good river, but very quiet, said the Chinese woman as they stepped onto the beautiful, green, rusting, slightly crumpled, totally unused pier and looked at New Jersey. They returned along a street of small houses and Faith pointed up to the second-floor apartment where she and Jack had first made love. Ah, the woman said, do you notice that in time you love the children more and the man less? Faith said, Yes! but as soon as she said it, she wanted to run home and find Jack and kiss his pink ears and his 243 last hairs, to call out, Old friend, don't worry, you are loved. But before she could speak of this, Tonto flew by on his financially rewarding messenger's bike, screaming, Hi, Mom, *nee hau, nee hau*. He has a Chinese girlfriend this week. He says that means hello. My other son is at a meeting. She didn't say it was the L.R.Y.'s regular beep-the-horn-if-you-support-Mao meeting. She showed her the church basement where she and Ruth and Ann and Louise and their group of mostly women and some men had made leaflets, offered sanctuary to draft resisters. They would probably do so soon again. Some young people looked up from a light board, saw a representative of the Third World, and smiled peacefully. They walked east and south to neighbor-hoods where our city, in fields of garbage and broken brick, stands desolate, her windows burnt and blind. Here, Faith said, the people suffer and struggle, their children turn round and round in one place, growing first in beauty, then in rage.

Now we are home again. And I will tell you about my life, the Chinese woman said. Oh yes, please, said Faith, very embarrassed. Of course the desire to share the facts and places of her life had come from generosity, but it had come from self-centeredness too.

The Expensive Moment

Yes, the Chinese woman said. Things are a little better now. They get good at home, they get a little bad, then improve. And the men, you know, they were very bad. But now they are a little better, not all, but some, a few. May I ask you, do you worry that your older boy is in a political group that isn't liked? What will be his trade? Will he go to university? My eldest is without skills to this day. Her school years happened in the time of great confusion and running about. My youngest studies well. Ah, she said, rising. Hello. Good afternoon.

Ruth stood in the doorway. Faith's friend, the listener and the answerer, listening.

We were speaking, the Chinese woman said. About the children, how to raise them. My youngest sister is permitted to have a child this year, so we often talk thoughtfully. This is what we think: Shall we teach them to be straightforward, honorable, kind, brave, maybe shrewd, self-serving a little? What is the best way to help them in the real world? We don't know the best way. You don't want them to be cruel, but you want them to take care of themselves wisely. Now my own children are nearly grown. Perhaps it's too late. Was I foolish? I didn't know in those years how to do it.

Yes, yes, said Faith. I know what you mean. Ruthy?

Ruth remained quiet.

Faith waited a couple of seconds. Then she turned to the Chinese woman. Oh, Xie Feng, she said. Neither did I.

Listening

I had just come up from the church basement with an armful of leaflets. Once, maybe only twenty-five, thirty years ago, young women and men bowled in that basement, played Ping-Pong there, drank hot chocolate, and wondered how in God's separating world they could ever get to know each other. Nowadays we mimeograph and collate our political pamphlets among the bowling alleys. I think I'm right when I remember that the leaflets in my arms cried out, *U.S. Honor the Geneva Agreements*. (Jack did not believe the U.S. would ever honor the Geneva Agreements. Well, then, sadness, Southeast Asian sadness, U.S. sadness, all-nation sadness.)

Then I thought: Coffee. Do you remember the Art Foods Deli? The Sudarskys owned it, cooked for us, served us, argued Europe Israel Russia Islam, played chess in the late evening on the table nearest the kitchen, and in order to persuade us all to com-

passion and righteousness exhumed the terrible
town of his youth—Dachau.

With my coffee, I ordered a sandwich named after
a neighbor who lives a few blocks away. (All sandwiches are so honored.) I do like the one I asked for
—Mary Anne Brewer—but I must say I really prefer
Selena and Max Retelof, though it's more expensive.
The shrimp is not chopped quite so fine, egg is
added, a little sweet red pepper. Selena and Max
were just divorced, but their sandwich will probably go on for another few years.

At the table next to mine, a young man leaned
forward. He was speaking to an older man. The
young man was in uniform, a soldier. I thought,
When he leaves or if I leave first, I'll give him a
leaflet. I don't want to but I will. Then I thought,
Poor young fellow, God knows what his experience
has been; his heart, if it knew, would certainly
honor the Geneva Agreements, but it would probably hurt his feelings to hear one more word about
how the U.S.A. is wrong again and how he is an
innocent instrument of evil. He would take it personally, although we who are mothers and have
been sweethearts—all of us know that "soldier" is
what a million boys have been forced to be in every
single one of a hundred generations.

Uncle Stan, the soldier boy was saying, I got to
tell you, we had to have a big wedding then,
Mamasan Papasan, everybody was there. Then I got
rotated. I wrote to her, don't think I didn't. She has
a nice little baby girl now. If I go back I'll surely see

her. But, Stan, basically I want to settle down. I already reenlisted once. It would be good if I got to be a construction worker. If you know someone, one of Tommy's friends. If you got a contact. Airfields or harbors—something like that. I could go over for a year or two now and then. She wouldn't want to come back here. Here's the picture, see? She has her old grandma, everybody's smiling, right? I'm not putting her down, but I would like to find a good-looking American girl, someone nice, I mean, and fall in love and settle down, because, you know, I'm twenty-four already.

Uncle Stan said, Twenty-four, huh? Then he asked for the check. Two coffees, two Helen someone or others. While the waitress scribbled, I, bravely, but against my better judgment, passed one of the leaflets to the young man. He stood up. He looked at it. He looked at me. He looked at the wall, sighing. Oh shit. He crumpled the leaflet in one hand. He looked at me again. He said, Oh, I'm sorry. He put the leaflet on the table. He smoothed it out.

Let's go, said Uncle Stan.

I'd finished my lunch, but Art Foods believes that any eating time is the body's own occasion and must not be hurried. In the booth behind me two men were speaking.

The first man said: I already have one child. I cannot commit suicide until he is at least twenty or twenty-two. That's why when Rosemarie says, Oh, Dave, a child? I have to say, Rosemarie, you deserve one. You do, you're a young woman, but no. My son (by Lucy) is now twelve years old. Therefore if things do not work out, if life does not show some meaning, MEANING by God, if I cannot give up drinking, if I become a terrible drunk and know I have to give it up but cannot and then need to commit suicide, I think I'd be able to hold out eight or nine years, but if I had another child I would then have to last twenty years. I cannot. I will not put myself in that position.

The other man said: I too want the opportunity, the freedom to commit suicide when I want to. I too assume that I will want to in ten, twenty years. However, I have responsibilities to the store, the men that work there. I also have my real work to finish. The one serious thing that would make me commit suicide would be my health, which I assume will deteriorate—cancer, heart disease, whatever. I refuse to be bedridden and dependent and therefore I am sustained in the right to leave this earth when I want to do so and on time.

The men congratulated each other on their unsentimentality, their levelheadedness. They said almost at the same time, You're right, you're right. I turned to look at them. A little smile just tickled the corners of their lips. I passed one of my leaflets over the back of the booth. Without looking up, they began to read.

Jack and I were at early-morning breakfast when I told him the two little stories. And Jack, I said, one of those men was you.

Well, he said, I know it was me. You don't have

to remind me. I saw you looking at us. I saw you listening. You don't have to tell stories to me in which I'm a character, you know. Besides which, all those stories are about men, he said. You know I'm more interested in women. Why don't you tell me stories told by women about women?

Those are too private.

Why don't you tell them to me? he asked sadly.

Well, Jack, you have your own woman stories. You know, your falling-in-love stories, your French-woman-during-the-Korean-War stories, your magnificent-woman stories, your beautiful-new-young-wife stories, your political-comrade-though-extremely-beautiful stories . . .

Silence—the space that follows unkindness in which little truths growl.

Then Jack asked, Faith, have you decided not to have a baby?

No, I've just decided to think about it, but I haven't given it up.

So, with the sweetness of old forgiving friendship, he took my hand. My dear, he said, perhaps you only wish that you were young again. So do I. At the store when young people come in waving youth's unfurled banner HOPE, meaning their pockets are full of someone's credit cards, I think: New toasters! Brand-new curtains! Sofa convertibles! Danish glass!

I hadn't thought of furniture from the discount store called Jack, Son of Jake as a song of beginnings. But I guess that's what it is—straw for the spring-time nest.

Now listen to me, he said. And we began to

address each other slowly and formally as people often do when seriousness impedes ease; some stately dance is required. Listen. Listen, he said. Our old children are just about grown. Why do you want a new child? Haven't we agreed often, haven't we said that it had become noticeable that life is short and sorrowful? Haven't we said the words "gone" and "where"? Haven't we sometimes in the last few years used the word "terrible" and we mean to include in it the word "terror"? Everyone knows this about life. Though of course some fools never stop singing its praises.

But they're right, I said in my turn. Yes, and this is in order to encourage the young whom we have, after all, brought into the world—they must not be abandoned. We must, I said, continue pointing out simple and worthwhile sights such as—in the countryside—hills folding into one another in light-green spring or white winter, the sky which is always astonishing either in its customary blueness or in the configuration of clouds—the way they're pushed in their softest parts by the air's breath and change shape and direction and density. Not to mention our own beloved city crowded with day and night workers, shoppers, walkers, the subway trains which many people fear but they're so handsomely lined with pink to dark dark brown faces, golden tans and yellows scattered amongst them. It's very important to emphasize what is good or beautiful so as not to have a gloomy face when you meet some youngster who has begun to guess.

Well, Jack said.

Then he said, You know, I like your paragraphs better than your sentences. That comment wasn't made (I knew) in order to set the two forms in hostile opposition. It was still part of the dance, a couple of awkward, critical steps from theory to practice.

Perhaps, he continued, if we start making love in the morning, your body will be so impressed and enlivened by the changes in me that it will begin again all its old hormonal work of secreting, womb cleaning, and egg making.

I doubt it, I said. Besides, I'm busy, you know. I have an awful lot to do.

By this, I meant that our early mornings are usually so full of reading last night's paper, dissenting and arguing appropriate actions, waking the boys, who should really be old enough to understand an alarm clock when it speaks to them—without their mother's translation. Also, we had once had the moral or utilitarian idea that brainy labor must happen early; it must precede the work of love or be damaged by the residual weight of all that damp reality.

But Jack said, Oh, come on. He unbuttoned his shirt. My face is very fond of the gray-brown hairs of his chest. Thanks, I said, but it won't work, you know. Miracles don't happen, and if they do they're absolutely explainable. He began to get a very rosy look about him, which is a nice thing to happen to a man's face. It's not called blushing. Blushing is an

expression of shyness and female excitement at the
same time. In men it's observed as an energetic act
the blood takes on its determined own.

Think think, talk talk, that's you, stop it! Come
on, kid, he said, touching my knee, my thigh, breast,
all the outsides of love. So we lay down beside one
another to make a child, with the modesty of later-
in-life, which has so much history and erotic knowledge but doesn't always use it.

How else is one to extract a new person from all-
refusing Zeus and jealous Hera? My God, said Jack,
you've never mentioned Greek gods in bed before.
No occasion, I said.

Later on he called the store to tell the salesmen
not to sell too many kitchen sets without him, he
couldn't afford to give away all that commission.
Wouldn't you think that would annoy the men?
Jack says I don't understand the way men talk to
one another.

I had just started the coffee when Richard, my
very large and handsome son, appeared. He is
known far and wide for his nosy ear. Why are you
still in your pajamas? I asked. He answered, What
is this crap, Mother, this life is short and terrible.
What is this metaphysical shit, what is this disease
you intelligentsia are always talking about.

First we said: Intelligentsia! Us? Oh, the way
words lie down under decades, then the Union of
Restless Diggers out of sheer insomnia pulls them
up: daggers for the young but to us they look like
flowers of nostalgia that grew in our mother's for-

eign garden. What *did* my mother say? Darling, you should have come to Town Hall last night, the whole intelligentsia was there. My uncle, strictly: The intelligentsia will never permit it!

So I laughed. But Jack said, Don't you dare talk to your mother like that, Richard! Don't you dare! Ma, Richard said, get his brains out of the pickle jar, it's no insult. Everyone knows, the intelligentsia strikes the spark, so that they'll be relevant for a long time, striking sparks here and there.

Of course, he explained, the fire of revolution would only be advanced, contained, and put to productive use by the working class. Let me tell you, Jack, the intelligentsia better realize this. And another thing, where'd you get that don't-dare-talk-to-my-mother stuff . . . I know her a lot longer than you do. I've been talking to her for maybe almost eighteen years and you've been sitting around our house maybe three years tops.

Sorry, Richard. I heard a character on a TV show last night say exactly that. "Don't you dare talk to your mother like that." I had gone over to see Anna about something. She turned on the TV the minute I came in.

Wow! Really? Listen, the same thing happened to me too. I went to see Caitlin, you know Caitlin, around the corner, the doctor's daughter. The one whose kid brother tried to set fire to the nun a couple of years ago? Well, you know, she did that too the minute I came in, she turned on the TV.

Huh! They were surprised that the girl and the

woman unknown to one another had done exactly the same thing to each of them. Richard offered Jack a cigarette and sat down at the kitchen table. Coffee, Ma, he said.

Then Jack asked, Richard, tell me, do you forgive your father for having run out on you kids years ago?

I don't forgive him and I don't not forgive him. I can't spend my life on personal animosities. The way imperialism's leaning so hard on the Third World the way it does . . .

Jack said, Ah . . . He blinked his eyes a couple of times, which a person who can't cry too well often does. Richard, did you know my father was a junk peddler. He had a pushcart. He yelled (in Yiddish), Buy old clothes, buy old clothes. I had to go with him, walk up to the fifth floor, pick up stuff; I guess we crawled up and down every street in the Bronx . . . Buy old clothes . . . old clothes.

Richard said, Oh!

What do you think, Jack asked. Rich, do you think my daughter, I mean Kimmy, will she ever call me up and say, It's O.K., Dad?

Well, said Richard, nodding his head, shrugging his shoulders.

I have to go to work now, I said. I don't happen to own my own business. Also, I have a late meeting tonight. O.K.?

The two men nodded. They sat quietly together expanding their lungs to the tiniest thread of tissue with smoke. Breathing deeply, dangerously, in and out.

. . .

Then, as often happens in stories, it was several years later. Jack had gone off to Arizona for a year to clear his lungs and sinuses and also to have, hopefully, one last love affair, the kind that's full of terrific longing, ineluctable attraction, and so forth. I don't mean to mock it, but it's only natural to have some kind of reaction. Lots of luck, Jack, I said, but don't come home grouchy. The boys were in different boroughs trying to find the right tune for their lives. They had been men to a couple of women and therefore came for supper only now and then. They were worried for my solitariness and suggested different ways I could wear my hair.

Of course, because of this planet, which is dropping away from us in poisonous disgust, I'm hardly ever home. The other day, driving down the West Side—Broadway—after a long meeting, I was stopped at a red light. A man in the absolute prime of life crossed the street. For reasons of accumulating loneliness I was stirred by his walk, his barest look at a couple of flirty teenage girls; his nice unimportant clothes seemed to be merely a shelter for the naked male person.

I thought, Oh, man, in the very center of your life, still fitting your skin so nicely, with your arms probably in a soft cotton shirt and the shirt in an old tweed jacket and your cock lying along your thigh in either your right or left pants leg, it's hard to tell which, why have you slipped out of my sentimental and carnal grasp?

He's nice, isn't he? I said to my friend Cassie.

I suppose so, she said, but Faith, what is he, just a bourgeois on his way home.

To everyday life, I said, sighing with a mild homesickness.

To whose everyday life, she said, goddamnit, whose?

She turned to me, which is hard to do when you're strapped and stuffed into a bucket seat. Listen, Faith, why don't you tell my story? You've told everybody's story but mine. I don't even mean my whole story, that's my job. You probably can't. But I mean you've just omitted me from the other stories and I was there. In the restaurant and the train, right there. Where is Cassie? Where is *my* life? It's been women and men, women and men, fucking, fucking. Goddamnit, where the hell is my woman and woman, woman-loving life in all this? And it's not even sensible, because we *are* friends, we work together, you even care about me at least as much as you do Ruthy and Louise and Ann. You let them in all the time; it's really strange, why have you left me out of everybody's life?

I took a deep breath and turned the car to the curb. I couldn't drive. We sat there for about twenty minutes. Every now and then I'd say, My God! or, Christ Almighty! neither of whom I usually call on, but she was stern and wouldn't speak. Cassie, I finally said, I don't understand it either; it's true, though, I know what you mean. It must feel for you like a great absence of yourself. How could I allow it. But it's not me alone, it's them too. I waited for her to say something. Oh, but it *is* my fault. Oh, but why did you wait so long? How can you forgive me?

Forgive you? She laughed. But she reached across the clutch. With her hand she turned my face to her so my eyes would look into her eyes. You are my friend, I know that, Faith, but I promise you, I won't forgive you, she said. From now on, I'll watch you like a hawk. I do not forgive you.